W9-DBF-359

Baseball, Bullies & Angels

by Daryl K. Cobb

10 To 2 Children's Book
Clinton

ISBN 978-0615879239
Library of Congress Control Number: 2013917866

10 To 2 Children's Books

Printed in the USA

This edition first printing, December 2013
Book design by Daryl K. Cobb

Also by Daryl K. Cobb:

Children's Novels:

Pirates: The Ring of Hope

Baseball, Bullies & Angels

Picture Books:

Bill the Bat Finds His Way Home

Daniel Dinosaur

Daddy Did I Ever Say? I Love You, Love You, Every Day

Bill the Bat Loves Halloween

Bill the Bat Baby Sits Bella

Boy on the Hill

Do Pirates Go To School?

Count With Daniel Dinosaur

Henry Hare's Floppy Socks

Barnyard Buddies: Perry Parrot Finds a Purpose

Pirates: Legend of the Snarlyfeet

Greta's Magical Mistake

Mr. Moon

The Frogs: A Happy Life

For Daryl's books,
music and author visit information:
www.darylcobb.com

A note from the author:

It is my hope that *Baseball, Bullies & Angels* will entertain you, that Charlie will make you laugh and you will relate to the characters and the situations they find themselves in. It was also my goal while writing this story to bring you into Stephen's life, the life of a bullying victim, and show you the highs and lows. I want you all to understand that bullying can happen to anyone, even a star baseball player.

We all know from reading or listening to the news that not all children can see past what is happening to them right now. There is no tomorrow, there is only today. As a child who struggled in school and was bullied until the age of fourteen, I know the feeling of desperation a child can experience when they can't see an end to their troubles, and I feel for anyone who is going through it.

Bullying is one of the most important topics in our society today. The damage it causes can have life-long ramifications. That is why I needed to tell this story. I hope it will reach in and grab you by the heartstrings. I think all kids need to understand the consequences that poor decision-making can have, as well as the impact it can have on your life, the lives of your family and friends and even on those people who aren't your favorites. How we treat others and how we are treated by others will define the people we will eventually become.

To Charlie 1961-2013

Table of Contents

Chapter 1

On Deck

Standing in the hitter's circle is my time to get my head completely into the game. There is no conversation with other players, it is just me. I swing a few times to loosen up and I concentrate on the only thing that is important, what is coming: my turn at bat. I watch each pitch that is being thrown. I watch for the pitcher's release point so I can start eyeing up the ball. I am getting into my zone and shutting down all other distractions. I hear everything but hear nothing. Not the chanting. Not the screaming. Nothing. It has all become background noise. The adrenaline is pumping and I am excited, nervous and scared all at the same time. I try not to think about the importance of this one particular at bat, and why this at bat is any different than any of the others. Why is it different? Because everything our team has worked for all season long is on the line, win or go home.

We are only down by two runs and we have the bases loaded so the game is ours for the taking. But in sports there are no guarantees, so many things can happen. For one, the batter could hit into a double play and the game would be over. I would be left on deck dreaming of what would have happened or what might have happened if I had gotten up to the plate one last time. But with no balls and two strikes against our batter my chances of getting that opportunity are looking really good. I'm Stephen Miller, and I'm on deck.

Chapter 2

Home Town

If you were a stranger driving through Lamington on any normal day you would probably pass through it and not give it any thought whatsoever. It's a nice enough town, I guess. I don't really have a lot to compare it to though since I haven't been to that many towns. It's quiet, at least most of the time. We do hear an occasional siren blasting out from the firehouse or a horn blowing from the New York bound commuter train. But despite these infrequent disturbances, it's quiet.

This small peaceful town is divided by one main street which is cleverly called Main Street and connects to the same highway at both ends. We have lots of little side streets which, in an aerial view, probably look like a maze. There are a lot of trees surrounding streets and houses, homes that were built and cemented into place decades ago. Some have even been standing since before the end of the Spanish-American War in 1898. But even though the houses are old, everyone here takes good care of them.

The residents of Lamington attend one of our three churches. I go to the Methodist church on most Sundays with my parents and annoying little brother Jack. We also have one for Catholics which is the biggest and fanciest of the three. Then there is the one for Presbyterians, which I have been trying to convince my brother to join so he doesn't pester me during the whole service. But if he joined the Catholic one it would make me just as happy.

There are no stop lights anywhere in town and only one gas station, Apgar's, where they spend the day fixing cars and pumping gas. They have a soda machine parked outside next to the waiting area door and inside they have an ice cream cooler where I get my root beer popsicles from. I love root beer: root beer barrels, root beer floats and my all-time favorite are root beer popsicles. Even with three convenience shops in town, Apgar's is still the only place you can buy them.

Lamington isn't known for its quaint little shops because there are none. It isn't known for any great contribution to our county history or the history of our country because none happened. It really isn't known for much of anything, and definitely not shopping. If people want that they can drive ten miles to Clinton, where every other building is a store, or they can go a little further to any one of the bigger towns of the many that surround us.

But that doesn't mean we don't have a few stores because we do. With the exception of Stanley's Printing and The Dipper, these stores are mostly small town versions of a 7-Eleven that are run out of the bottom level of an old two-story Victorian house with the owners living one floor above. All three of Lamington's convenience stores sell pretty much the same things like milk, bread, ketchup, sugar, etc., things that you might need to pick up on the fly if Mom

runs out. Now I don't know why anyone needs three of the same kind of store in one little town but that's what we have.

The only store that dares to be different is The Dipper. This store is run by the Cabbells and, like I said, it's not in a house. Mr. Cabbell is a teacher like my dad and spent one entire summer constructing his little ice cream palace in his side yard. The building is a small rectangle, a cinder block box with a front and back door and a sliding window like you see at the drive-thru of McDonald's. When he finished up the construction he painted the store midnight blue and stuck a big metal post in the ground in front of it with a lighted sign that says "The Dipper". A lot of the town's people think it's an eyesore but the kids love it. Plus they grill and deep fry food so the smell of burgers and fries is always in the air. I love that smell! They also sell convenience items but it's the food from the grill and hand-dipped ice cream that makes them popular. And on top of that it gives us kids a place to hang out.

Hanging out at The Dipper is part of our everyday lives, like brushing your teeth. It's something that we all do, with some doing it longer and more often than others. Mr. Cabbell isn't always happy with the amount of lounging around going on; he calls it "loitering" and often chases away the kids that over-stay their welcome. But like bees to a hive we always come buzzing back.

I guess the good thing about having three of these stores in your town is that you don't have to walk far to get what you need (my mom says that's why they're called *convenience* shops). If you live on my side of town you have Apgar's Garage and The Dipper. If you live in the center of town you have Shaller's and the printing shop. And people at the far end can make a stop at Shorty's Mom & Pop and then walk over to the post office to send out their mail. It is conveniently set up for all.

If you decide to take the scenic route and weave your way through the maze of streets in our town, you will eventually either drive by or stop next to my house. It really just depends what direction you're coming from. My house is located on a corner lot where Moore Street connects to New Street, house number 23. We are right next to the Alpaughs who are cousins of the Apgars who own the gas station where I get my root beer popsicles. And my best friend Charlie lives right across the road from me.

As you go down New Street just a few miles you will pass right by Lamington Public School, which was built nearly one hundred years ago. That is where I go to school. I'm a seventh grader there and my friend Charlie is in eighth. In the old days the school used to go all the way through high school. Charlie's dad even went there. His dad told me once that his ninth grade class was the last ninth graders to attend Lamington Public. After that, Lamingtion Public ninth graders went to the new regional high school, where I'll go in a couple of years.

On any given Monday of the school year you would normally find most of us kids in that school, dads working and the moms doing mom things. Some of the moms in town also work but they're the minority. Most of the moms in Lamingtown don't work and spend the day doing things around their houses and in their yards. During the day shopping gets done, dishes get washed, and houses get cleaned, all those everyday things that we tend to take for granted (as my mom likes to point out), the mom fairy takes care of. But today is not a normal Monday. It is Memorial Day and schools are closed.

Memorial Day, as I have been told, is a day of reflection, a day that the people of our country honor the men and women who died in the armed services; in wars, basically. And like all Memorial Days before this one, it is on a Monday. Well, just to clarify, when I say "all" what I mean to say is, all Memorial Days in my lifetime. Because the holiday has been celebrated since 1868, which is like 130 years before I was born. It was also called Decoration Day until 1967 and celebrated on May 30th, which didn't always fall on a Monday. I think the first time it was celebrated on a Monday was in 1971. As a matter of fact I am positive it was 1971 because I just looked it up.

I'm not normally good with facts and dates unless those facts have something to do with baseball, but as it turns out, these facts do. This may not be true for everyone but for me they do. In Lamington, Memorial Day is also the first day of baseball season.

Chapter 3

Baseball Season

In Lamington, Memorial Day kicks off a sixteen game schedule where our town's eight teams all battle each other trying to get to the Little League World Series. In this sleepy little town only one thing zaps it to life and wakes everyone up out of their stupors, and that's baseball. Our town becomes a bustling madhouse on opening day of baseball season. People crawl out from every crack and crevice to watch our games. All those people that disappeared off the radar screen in the fall and winter now reappear. Residents you thought had moved away sneak back home. Lamington also organizes one of the biggest parades in the county and we all like being part of it. So on this day of the year, the town opens its doors and the people come flooding in. It is baseball season so let the day begin!

The festivities in town start at eight in the morning with the parade up Main Street, so if you're coming be prepared for parking problems and have your walking shoes on. The parade participants, which includes me, start lining up at the firehouse on Wells Avenue and by the time they finish, the line runs halfway down the street.

The parade moves quickly from the corner of Wells Avenue onto Main Street and then right up the hill. Along our route the spectators fill the sidewalks and the residents that aren't in the parade all sit out on their porches and watch. At the top of the hill we take a sharp curve, passing the Catholic church and Apgar's, and we make a quick right onto New Street. The parade moves right past my house where my mom and dad wait to wave at me. After I see them we keep going right past the park until we eventually spill out onto the ball fields.

People of all ages participate in the parade including groups of veterans from every war dressed up in their uniforms. There are fire trucks from different eras, a few rescue squads, the high school band and twirling squad, the boy scouts, the girl scouts, the girls' softball teams and then all eight little league baseball teams dressed in our new-for-this-year uniforms. We wear our hats proudly, anxious for what the day will bring: baseball!

Memorial Day and baseball always seem to go together, like Pepsi and pizza. Well, that's what I like anyway. If that doesn't work for you then how about cookies and milk. I kind of think of it this way: this day honors those people who died in battle fighting for us, so it is only because of them that we are able to step onto the ball field and play today. So in their memory our teams take to the fields to battle one another. Think of it as a Civil War reenactment done in a fun way without the death part.

Is it disrespectful to do something fun on a day we are paying respect to people who gave their lives for us? I hope not. But I figure it isn't something I should worry about. I'm a kid and the adults are running the show so it must be okay, right?

On Memorial Day the games are played throughout the day with the minor leaguers playing on the small field and the major league boys playing on the regulation size one. Lights were installed a few year ago on the majors field courtesy of the Lamington Athletic Commission so some games now go into the evening.

The lights were a great addition to the ball field but did cause some grumbling in town from some parents and coaches in the minor leagues. The Commission's thinking at the time was that the little kids wouldn't be playing late enough in the evening to require lights but some of those parents disagreed. Despite the grumbles it was a nice thing to do and now, because of the lights, darkness is never an issue for me and my team.

Having the last game of the day is a little bit of a letdown actually with the excitement of the parade and all. When we got to the fields I just wanted to get out there and play. But like they say sometimes, we were all dressed up with no place to go. Whether we like it or not the Giants will have to wait. That's who I play for and we got the 7pm time slot this year.

Having the last game of the day does have one advantage: it is the only game on the schedule that doesn't have a time limit. You just play until the game is done. The day games all have to be played within a two hour window and when the time is up so is your game. If you only got four innings in, tough.

So the bad part today will be the wait, but the good thing is my friend Charlie, who I told you lives across the street from me, has the five o'clock game so we have almost the whole day to kill together.

"So what do you want to do? I don't have to be back here until four," Charlie said to me when the parade ended.

"I don't know, what do you want to do?"

"We could see if Linda Mohoney is working the snack shack."

"She's in high school. Why would she be working the snack shack?"

Linda is a legend in town. She isn't much older than us but she's beautiful and famous. She just signed with the Ford Modeling Agency in Manhattan. That's in New York City. I don't have any experience with modeling but I was told Ford is one of the biggest agencies in the country.

"I hear she needs community service hours," Charlie answered.

"How would you know?"

"My sister told me."

"And how would she know?"

"She heard my mom talking to your mom."

"So it must be true," I said rolling my eyes.

My mom loves to gossip but sometimes I think she makes stuff up just to keep life interesting. Not big stuff, just little unimportant things like who might be working in the snack shack. But it was a rumor that was at least worth checking into despite its source.

"You want to check it out?"

"I am getting a little hungry," I said with a smile.

"Let's get some hot dogs," Charlie said.

"I don't want hot dogs," I said, kind of surprised.

"Why not?"

"It's 9am."

"So what?"

"It's 9am, that's so what. I don't eat hot dogs for breakfast."

"Hot dogs are just like bologna," Charlie informed me.

"I don't eat bologna for breakfast either."

"Really?"

"No." I made a face.

"Why not? It's just like pork roll."

"It's nothing like pork roll."

"If you fry it it is."

"It is not. Pork roll is made from pork and bologna is made from…" I had to stop and think about it for a second. "I don't know what it's made from but it's not pork."

"It *is* made from pork. You can get it in beef, turkey and chicken too, but the kind my mom gets is pork."

"You're kidding right?"

"I'm not. You really have never had it fried?"

"No, have you?" I said.

"All the time."

"Really?" I said, not believing him.

"Really, and it's good!"

"And people eat that for breakfast?" I was still skeptical.

"They do, and if people eat it for breakfast then it counts as breakfast food, am I right?"

"I guess so."

"I know so!" said Charlie claiming his victory.

"Okay then. Let's get hot dogs!" I said enthusiastically, but when I searched my back pocket I realized … . "You know what? My mom didn't give me any money."

"I'll pay and you can pay me back later."

"Okay, thanks. Get me two hot dogs with mustard, raw onion and pickles. I've got to use the bathroom," I said. "I've been holding it in now for an hour and I'm about to burst."

"Raw onions and pickles?" Charlie said frowning.

"What's wrong with onion and pickles?"

"No one eats raw onions and pickles for breakfast."

Chapter 4

Partners in Crime

I don't know what it is about Charlie but he and I just seem to click. We are partners in crime my mom would say. We do pretty much everything together. Like last summer we took a bike trip and my dad even let him come camping with us, which was a lot more fun than going with just my brother.

Every year my dad takes me and my brother Jack on a two week camping trip but after a few days it gets a little boring. Who wants to spend two weeks with just your little brother? So last year Dad let us each invite one person to come with us. Jack chose his friend Warren who he hangs out with during band practice and I brought Charlie.

This arrangement worked out great. My dad would go fishing early in the morning with my uncle, leaving all us kids behind with my grandfather. Gramps didn't like getting up early and that worked fine for us since we could all pretty much do what we wanted.

So while my dad and uncle fished, Jack and Warren did whatever band people like to do and Charlie and I went down to the dock

area to swim. At first I wasn't happy when I learned we had to share the dock with the family in the cabin next to us. I thought it was just going to be me and Charlie. I knew Charlie didn't mind but I am always a little uncomfortable around strangers and it felt like an invasion of my privacy. My dad told me that there wasn't anything he could do so live with it, but I still didn't want to hang out with boys I didn't know. That was until those boys turned out to be two sisters from Suffern, New York, who liked to dive off of the dock in their bikinis. We spent the whole two weeks with these girls swimming, hanging out and getting to know each other. When it came time to leave we were all a little sad so we swapped phone numbers and e-mails. It made going our separate ways easier knowing we could all keep in touch.

I don't think we were home for more than a few days when Charlie and I were sitting on the front porch steps at my house talking about the girls and we came up with this great idea: a road trip! The girls only lived in Suffern, New York, which was about sixty-five miles from our houses. That was like right down the street; we couldn't believe how close they lived. Okay, so it's a little further than down the street but it was still close. So we figured we'd surprise the girls by going there to visit. It was way better than e-mailing back and forth. I mean, we would do that too but this would be way more fun. So we decided that we'd pack a lunch, get on our bikes and pedal our way to see them.

We told our moms that day that we were going out to ride our bikes and we'd be back before dinner. It wasn't anything unusual since we do this all the time. Our parents didn't worry too much because we live in a small town; where could we possibly go? The one rule was that no matter what we were doing we had to be home and ready for dinner at six.

With the thought of the girls as the only thing in our heads, we started out the trip really excited, pedaling hard and fast, trying to make good time. But we soon discovered that it wasn't going to be as easy as we anticipated. We'd get a good pace going and then the road would slope uphill a little and slow us down, and then we'd hit a steeper hill and we'd be crawling along at a snail's pace. Of course we made up lots of time going downhill but eventually it would flatten out and we'd slow down again.

The part of the trip I really hated was Schooley's Mountain. When you go up this mountain in a car it doesn't look like it would be that hard to bike up, but let me tell you, I almost died. My legs were fried halfway up and we both thought we should throw in the towel and just go home. But instead we battled it out all the way to the top, and we were glad we did. Because once we hit the peak we were able to coast back down the other side for miles without ever having to pedal. The mountain got so steep at times that we had to use the brakes to slow down. We were having so much fun now that it didn't even cross our minds that we would have to ride back up; we were flying high and having fun letting go of the handle bars with our arms stretched out like the wings of a plane. The speed was exciting and the air hitting our faces felt good, and we just enjoyed it for as long as it lasted. When the mountain eventually leveled off we went back to pedaling again.

After we came down the other side of Schooley's Mountain we

went through the business section of one of those big towns that moms shop at. We had been in this town many times before, but it was always in a car. When you see things from a car it's like watching a movie with the volume turned off. Things are happening right in front of your eyes but you don't feel or hear anything so it doesn't seem real somehow.

It's not like that on a bike. While you're pedaling along you can feel the whole world around you. The birds are chirping, dogs barking, and we heard the bubbling rushing water from the stream that ran along the side of the road. It was those sounds and the smell of the outdoors that made your senses come alive. We were no longer spectators locked into the cockpit of a car. It was an amazing feeling and we didn't want it to end.

But by two o'clock that good feeling was gone and we both started to feel nauseous. We weren't sure why, maybe from the heat or the lack of food, but we both knew we had to stop and take a break. We had gone pretty far up to that point and were now pedaling on the shoulder of interstate Route 80 (most people just call it I-80). When we stopped Charlie quickly took out his map and calculated that we had biked a whopping thirty-seven miles. This news gave us both a little more energy because we only had twenty-eight miles to go.

Charlie had figured that I-80 would save us lots of time but I didn't like that there was nowhere to sit and eat. The lucky thing was it did have steel guardrails along the shoulder. I guess they're to keep the cars from driving off the road, but we used it to lean our bikes against.

There was a lot more traffic on I-80 than what we had run into so far and we didn't see any other people standing or walking on it. But it also dawned on me, as I thought about it, even when I was in my parent's car I never really noticed people walking or biking on it. That was probably because there was no place to sit, plus all the tractor trailers whizzing by us made it hard to hear each other talk. So I could see why it wouldn't be a popular spot for people without cars.

Since there were no other seating options the guardrail seemed like the best place to sit as well. With the temperature topping ninety degrees and the sun beating down on us the rail was so hot we could feel it burning through our shorts. There was no shade and we both agreed that it would have been much better if we had eaten earlier when we could have parked ourselves under a nice tree. At least that would have gotten us out of the sun for a little while. Of all the August days we could have taken this journey we picked probably the hottest one, and by the end of lunch we had not only eaten all of our food but we had drained every drop of water too.

We did get a little relief from the heat with all the summer traffic because all those passing vehicles were creating a nice little breeze. When the tractor trailers flew by us at eighty miles an hour it was more like gusty winds, but it felt nice.

With lunch done Charlie went back to the map to check his calculations. The trip so far had taken us five hours and the lunch break added another thirty minutes. As Charlie double-checked mileage and times, we realized that if we kept going we probably wouldn't get to Suffern until after eight o'clock. Now this was troubling for two reasons. The first was, if the girls' parents were anything like ours, they would probably be mad at us for showing up at their door at that late hour to visit and yell at us. Neither one of us wanted to get yelled at. The second reason was the most concerning though, and that was because if we didn't go back now we'd be lucky if we got home in time for breakfast, let alone dinner.

* * *

"Stephen, you're never going to believe this," Charlie said, returning from the snack shack holding four hot dogs and two cans of soda, one tucked under each armpit.

"What?"

"My mom just gave me money so you don't owe me anything for the hot dogs!" Charlie said all excited as he handed me my food.

"Thanks, but why did she give you extra money?"

"I told her I donated mine to the rescue squad."

"And she believed you?"

"Sure," he said, just a matter of fact.

"Really?" I said.

"Why not? I never lie," Charlie said with his mouth stuffed full of food.

* * *

I am sure that you have already figured out that getting home in three hours was going to be hard to do when we were five hours away. But that is in biking hours, not car hours, which is the only reason I didn't say getting home was going to be impossible.

Now between the two of us, Charlie had a lot more to worry about than me. If we had to measure the amount of trouble someone would be in, Charlie was way off the scale. My parents were easy-going and were more likely to lecture me on the need for proper decision making where Charlie's mom was more of the emotional type and would hit the roof, she would be so steamed.

Unlike my mom who was your typical American girl type, born and raised in southern New Jersey, Charlie's mom was European, with the Arnold Schwarzenegger-like accent and all. When she got angry and started to yell, she was scary. Really scary.

My mom said that her bark was worse than her bite, but if a pit bull were barking at you would you still walk into its yard? So I guess it shouldn't have surprised me when Charlie pulled out a Swiss Army knife and walked over to my bike and punctured the tire. It was lucky for him that the Rockaway Mall, which was one of those jumbo malls with tons of stores, was located right behind us off the highway. Just a short walk and we were at a telephone.

Yes, I said telephone. Neither Charlie nor I have the luxury of owning smart phones, or even regular cell phones that you can only use for calls. Both of our parents are on the same line of thinking that the less technology we have the better. They also don't see the need for us to have cell phones when we have a phone in every room of the house, and because when we aren't at home, either our moms or dads are usually with us.

Now, I said it was lucky for him it was a short walk to the mall because he was pushing my bike as I rode his. On the way to the mall he apologized for the tire and said he would pay for it, which I thought was a nice thing to do considering what he just did. The one thing that Charlie knew that I didn't think about was if he had called his mom for a ride, she would not only have been angry but she would have made him walk all the way back home just to punish him. So instead we came up with a great story to tell my mom and believe it or not she was surprisingly sympathetic. She picked us up in front of the mall some fifty minutes later, probably still in shock that we had ridden our bikes so far. In her mind, as long as we were together and we took the back roads it wasn't really such a big deal; it was more of an achievement. Even better news was that Charlie made it home for dinner with time to spare.

* * *

"What do you say we take another road trip to Suffern again this summer?"

"I don't think so." I looked sideways over at Charlie to see if he was joking with me.

"Why not?"

"If I remember it right, we didn't make it there the first time."

"That's because you got a flat tire."

"Is that how you remember it?"

"You did get a flat tire, didn't you?"

"Yes, but …"

"So if you were to take a lie detector test and they asked if you got a flat tire on I-80, what would you say?"

"Yes, but …"

"There are no buts on a lie detector test. You only answer yes or no. 'Stephen, were you home with Linda Mohoney on the night in question?' 'Yes.' 'Did you kill your wife?' 'No.' 'Did you get a flat tire on I-80?' 'Yes.'"

"You're nuts."

"Maybe so, but the answer is still YES!"

"The answer is NO, I do not want to try that again."

"But if we leave earlier this time we could make it."

"Charlie, do you remember why we were the only people on bikes on I-80?"

"Because it's illegal."

"That is correct."

"But we didn't know that at the time."

"But we do now."

"Back roads, there must be back roads," Charlie said, almost pleading. "I think we could take Route 46 through Rockaway this time."

"I don't think so."

"Come on, if we get tired we'll just go knock on Miss Stanton's door and ask her for a ride home. I heard she lives up that way." Charlie was clearly amused with himself by the way he said this.

"That is not funny."

"Sure it is."

"It's not and you know it." Miss Stanton is one of my teachers

and I don't think she likes me.

"Okay, sorry. Did she give you back your test yet?" Charlie said as he continued to chomp away on his food.

"Not yet."

"How do you think you did?"

"I studied for it."

"I didn't ask you that. I asked how you think you did."

"I don't really know, it could go either way."

"Which way are you anticipating it going?

"Same way it always goes."

"So you failed it?"

"I don't know that I failed it."

"So what happens to you if you fail it?"

"Summer school."

"That's no big deal, so you do a couple extra weeks in school and then you'll be able to move on to eight grade."

"I hate it though," I said.

"Look on the bright side, Linda Mohoney will be at the school doing her service hours this summer."

"How do you know that?"

"My mom told me."

"And who told her?"

"Your mom."

"So it must be true." I tried to not roll my eyes this time.

"Of course," Charlie said with a smile.

"Do you think there's a chance?"

"Probably not."

I knew Charlie was right. Why would she want to waste her summer working at the school.

"I take it she wasn't at the snack shack," I said.

"No, Margie Winkle's mom had it covered, but she's looking pretty hot herself."

"Charlie, that's gross."

"Why is that? I am a man, she's a woman."

"She's Margie's mom and you are a boy," I corrected.

"Man."

"Boy!" I said one more time.

"Well, we all can't be the 'man boy' like you. Isn't that what your mom's calling you now, the man boy!" Charlie said, laughing.

"Shut up."

Chapter 5

The Man Boy

I guess most people would consider me just a typical thirteen year old with typical teenage problems. But I am not really typical. For one, I'm six foot two. My mom calls me 'the man boy'. I know, that is just what Charlie said and it's true. She doesn't say it in a mean way or anything; I've known her all my life and she doesn't have a mean bone in her body. She is just calling it like she sees it, and I am a boy in a big man body.

But despite my size, I am just a kid. I think like a kid, I act like a kid and I feel things like a kid. And sometimes I get weighed down by certain feelings, and it's hard for me to believe that those feelings and the experiences that cause them won't last forever. It seems that way because in a kid's world time seems infinite. Wow, I like that word: infinite. I don't usually use words like that and I'm surprised I even used it in the right context. I guess it would be a good time to tell you that I struggle a lot in school so using words like "infinite" is a big deal for me. But I do like the sound of that word and I think it fits here because when I think of infinite I think of being at the beach and looking out at the ocean where there is no end in sight, and that is the way time feels to a kid: infinite.

Now the feeling of endless time isn't such a bad thing always, like when we are all having fun and life is coasting along happily, like a day at a water park. I know that certainly could go on forever, am I right? I mean who wouldn't like that! We'd get out of the water at the end of the day and look like aliens from the Planet Prune, but who would care if we were giant prune people. We had fun!

But there are other times when things in life get hard and you just want that awful feeling to go away. Take my brother Jack for example. He is smart as a whip but he can't hit a baseball. Every time he strikes out he feels bad and the longer it goes on the worse he feels. It's weighing on him and it is all he can think about sometimes. The kid wants to be like all the other boys playing ball, he just wants a hit. This might seem like a really stupid thing to be getting upset about but to a kid this is a huge deal.

If I had to compare it to an adult situation maybe it's like how my dad felt when he lost my mom's wedding ring. For the longest time that was all he seemed to talk about. We all have things that bother us and sometimes these little things seem like the end of the world.

I know that I am young and compared to world hunger and stuff my problems are flea-sized. But in my world they don't feel so small and, even for a big guy like me, sometimes the weight of those problems are crushing and more than I can handle. When I start to feel this kind of heavy pressure I go to my dad. Sometimes my mom, but my dad has this way about him that puts me at ease so I usually go to him. I don't have any idea most of the time what I am going to say to him and sometimes I don't say much of anything, but I go anyway.

Now, some people would question his methods (I know my mom does), but they work for me and I think he knows that. I will go up to him and he will put his hand on my shoulder, then he'll tap me on the back, pick up a baseball and two gloves and say, "Stephen, follow me."

He takes me out to our backyard, no matter what time of year it is (and I mean that too). We have had to actually shovel pathways through the snow, but we go outside and we toss the ball back and forth. I know this doesn't sound like it would solve anyone's problems, but the throwing is just part of Dad's therapy. The throwing relaxes me and puts me in a comfortable place and the next thing I know I am telling him things that I would normally keep to myself. I'm not usually big on sharing how I feel and it's not an easy thing for me to do. And I don't know about you but I find it harder to talk to my parents about that kind of stuff than to anyone. Maybe because I feel like they might judge me or think I am stupid or childish or, worse, I might say something that is embarrassing. I hate when that happens, so if I don't share I don't have to worry about it. But when we are throwing the ball around the world seems right and it seems okay to let a few things out. Plus, he and I love baseball.

I really love baseball. I love to watch it, I love to play it, and I even love to practice. My mom says that if I put half the amount of energy into school work as I do baseball I would probably do better.

Dad says that's her way of trying to motivate me, and that she is not trying to hurt my feelings. But school is a sore subject and sometimes it's hard to not take it personally.

Just imagine how you would feel if you studied for hours only to wake up the next day after all that work and you couldn't remember any of the material. Or imagine you walk away from a test thinking, "Wow, I did good on this one!" only to get it back later and find out you flunked it. Well, that is how school is going for me so, all things considered, I would much rather be on a baseball field than anywhere.

I have always seemed right at home on a ball field and it's been that way since I was little. Dad says that I took to baseball like ducks take to water. That from the moment I slipped on my first baseball glove he could tell I had a gift. I used to think he was just saying that because he was my dad and that is what all dads tell their kids. I once heard Bart Taller's dad tell him how good he was one day, and Bart would have had better luck catching a rabbit than a baseball. But it eventually became clear even to me that I could do things on a baseball field that most kids couldn't. So in one way my mother is right, if somehow I could get as good at school as I am at baseball then I could very well do better. Unfortunately that is a big if, because school on a good day for me is next to impossible.

Each school year I start out thinking that this is the year I am going to do well. I am going to go into class, listen carefully and absorb everything like a sponge. But that dream lasts for about the first ten minutes. As soon as the teacher gets getting going on something I start to drift away. My brain gets all foggy, almost like I've been hypnotized by a magician. The magician then transports me out of class and puts me down somewhere else. It's like in those Star Trek movies where the transporter sets you down on some unknown planet, but with me that planet is usually the baseball field. In this foggy state my mind starts to play out scenarios of games. Sometimes it's games that my team is about to play, but mostly I am replaying games I have already played.

My dad says that concentrating in school is no different than staying focused during a ball game; just keep your head in the game. But for some reason it doesn't work the same for me at school as it does on the field. Concentrating and focusing during class is just hard for me to do. I have the same problem when I am reading.

I will be reading along just fine and as I am finishing up the paragraph I realize that in my head I am just saying the words. I am reading them -- I can even hear myself saying them -- but each word is coming to me with no meaning. They are all just random words as if I were reading a vocabulary list. I finish my reading and remember nothing. So I start from the top and begin again but with each try it's the same result. After a few failed attempts I toss the book aside in frustration and my mind then goes to the only place in my life that seems to work perfectly, the baseball field.

Chapter 6

Back in the Game

A's VS. Giants

Like I said, my mind works totally different on a ball field than it does at school. When I am playing baseball, my focus never strays from the game. I have never found myself on a baseball field thinking about dividing fractions or who the twenty-second president of the United States was. My head is always in the game. And if I am thinking of anything beyond the moment it is strategy, how are we going to get each man out or how am I going to hit this pitcher or that pitcher. I am always thinking during the game but it is about what needs to be done to win. Plus, as a catcher, there is always something to be thinking about. I just wish school could be the same.

In school I can't seem to find a way to win. The teachers think that I am just lazy and don't want to do the work. At least that is what they are telling my parents. And after years of battling with me my parents are frustrated because they don't know what to do. My teachers are frustrated and seem to have given up on me, and I am more frustrated than all of them.

I work as hard or harder than a lot of kids, I really do. But

normal things that most people take for granted, like concentrating and listening, I don't do well. I don't know why this is, but I don't. One second I am listening just fine and then BOOM, I'm gone. My head gets that foggy thing going, like I've said, and then that little magician shows up and zaps me right onto the baseball field. Like right now my body is in my math class and Miss Stanton is going over fractions. (Math, by the way, is my least favorite subject and the funny thing is that my dad is a high school math teacher.) But that is only where my body is. My mind, well, right now we are up by two in the bottom of the last inning in last night's game and we need only two outs to finish the A's off and win the season opener.

"Stephen." Miss Stanton is looking right at me. "Are you with us on this?"

"Yes," I said, "I think so." It doesn't take much to bring me back either, just a few words.

"Good, can we move on to chapter six?"

"Sure," I said, like I really have some say in the matter.

Miss Stanton is like a guard dog. She doesn't miss anything in her class so I know she was well aware that I wasn't paying attention. And I am also sure she knew that I had no idea what she was talking about. Chapter six? "Chapter six in what?" is what I should have asked her.

I took a quick glance around the room only to discover that we were no longer working on math. In fact, I am the only one in class with a math book out. This means only one thing: we had moved on to history. As I switch books I hope that I don't attract attention to myself, but the muffled laughter tells me that it didn't go unnoticed by some of the other kids either.

My classmates are another sore subject. It isn't all of them, but there is a group of them I call the bully gang and they enjoy making my life miserable. Right now they have a campaign going to see just how far they can push and bend me before I break. So they all get great satisfaction when Miss Stanton catches me in my classroom comas, my spaced out journeys, or whatever you want to call my little lapses.

These whatever-you-call-them are creating bigger problems for me. I've fallen so far behind the other students that, with less than four weeks left of school, it is now next to impossible for me to get caught up. My parents have been setting up meetings with teachers to talk about ways to bring my grades up so I can just move on to eighth grade. Their suggestions include staying after school every day as well as the need for summer school.

I hate summer school and my parents know it too so this has now become their threat of choice -- the dreaded summer school. This threat, of course, is supposed to get me to buckle down and apply myself, (like I wasn't applying myself!), but let's face it; I am going to summer school. I know it. They know. It is as clear as the sun rising and setting each day.

I hadn't missed a year without summer school since first grade (only because they don't have summer school for kindergarten) and this year wouldn't be any different. But my parents would not give up the fight, they keep encouraging me to do better. And then there is *the talk*. It's the same talk every year about how we all learn at different paces and that I will eventually start to put it all together.

I just have to try harder.

But I was trying and it wasn't coming to me. To make matters worse, I was labeled: teacher's think that I'm lazy and my classmates see me as the slow kid. I am treated differently and I don't like it. It doesn't feel good. A student should be made to feel like they are special, like they are an important part of the class, but I just feel like an unwanted house guest.

The only place I feel like I am important and that I make a difference to anyone is on a baseball field. Not a single coach I have ever played for cared whether or not I was smart or dumb as a stump, they accepted me for who I was, who I am. I am eager to learn and love to practice which in a coach's eyes makes me valuable.

As the years have passed my skills have only gotten better and better. I am now at a point where my true abilities have separated me even further from the kids that I am playing with. And I am a big kid, I'm a man boy as my mom says. But even though I am big and getting bigger, it doesn't slow me down. I'm as quick and agile as most little guys. You know the ones that you see zip around the soccer fields with endless amounts of energy and wonder how they can keep going? Well that's me, but the Mac Truck-size version.

"Okay, does everyone have their book open to chapter six? Stephen, did you find where we are?"

"Yes, Miss Stanton."

"Good. Danny, would you mind reading the first paragraph for me."

"Yes, Ma'am. I mean no, Ma'am, I don't mind. 'In 1804 Lewis

and Clark…'"

It didn't take long before Danny's reading about Lewis and Clark sent me to my happy place. My team still had only one out, but now the A's had the bases loaded with the winning run standing by on first base.

Billy DeSanto was pitching and had run into a bit of trouble. My mom referred to Billy as Stick Boy, (but not so anyone could hear her though), and she wasn't being mean either. Billy was just a little on the thin side and, at the moment, Stick Boy was having lots of trouble finding the strike zone. Billy was usually "the man," our go-to guy; he had gotten us out of countless situations in the past. But now he was busy digging himself a hole. With each pitch that hole kept getting deeper and deeper, so deep in fact that he was going to have trouble climbing out.

Billy got the first out easily but then gave up a single to shallow center and proceeded to walk the next two batters to load the bases. He was slowly losing confidence in himself and he was having trouble zeroing in on the strike zone. The one spot he could find, which was the outside corner, the umpire just would not give him.

A person's body language can speak volumes and Billy's was screaming, "Take me out!" He was called Stick Boy because he was thin, but he was also very tall (not as tall as me but close), and as Billy stood on the mound kicking dirt, he was all hunkered over which made him look five inches shorter. He kept looking over at the dugout hoping that the coach would yank him out, but that was not going to happen. Billy had to finish out the game, win or lose, and we all knew it. Unfortunately, the A's knew it too. With our next game only a day away, Dell Haver (who is our best pitcher) was not an option and the rest of our pitchers had all hit their maximum pitch count. Billy was it, there was no one else left. Plus it always took Dell at least an inning to loosen up and get into a groove and we certainly didn't have an inning for Dell to find himself. Billy was just going to have to dig down and pull this one out.

We all knew that the next batter was going to be the toughest one. Billy had problems throwing to lefties and the A's only lefty batter was now up. I think if I were coaching the other team I would have just sent all my batters to the plate batting lefty whether they could hit that way or not. I would bet my 2009 Yankees World Series hat that Billy would walk most of them. I guess it was a good thing the other team's coach didn't think like me.

Billy was kicking at the dirt near the pitching rubber, moving it around. It was as if he were fluffing his pillow before dropping his head down to sleep. But then he planted his foot right in the middle of it and stared in my direction. Stick Boy was looking for a sign, like I was going to put down the number for some miracle pitch that would get him out of this mess. But there was no miracle pitch. And Billy had only one that was even coming close to the strike zone, a fastball, so that is the sign he got. He shook his head and launched his first pitch which crossed the plate inside and tight. Maybe just a little too tight because it sent the batter sprawling backwards into the dirt to avoid getting hit.

"Ball," the umpire yelled.

The second pitch was two feet over the batter's head.

"Ball two," the umpire said.

The third pitch found the outside corner. I held my glove locked into place without even flinching so the umpire could see where the pitch had crossed the plate. The umpire called it a ball anyway and I could see Billy roll his eyes and take off his hat.

Billy always played with his hat when he got frustrated. He'd take it off and put it on, take it off and put it on, finding a different position for it on his head each time. It was like his skull suddenly grew or shrunk so that he couldn't get it to fit right. But after a few minutes of hat play and a sharp warning from the umpire, Billy took the mound and delivered his next pitch. This one crossed the plate in the same location as the previous pitch, with the same result.

"Ball four," the umpire called out. "Take your base!"

Groans and moans erupted from the Giants' fans as well as some verbal protests, which parents are not supposed to do by the way. At the same time the fans for the A's all cheered as the runners advanced and a run walked in, cutting our lead down to one. With the winning run now standing on second you could sense the momentum switching direction. Billy was like a runaway train that was destined to crash.

I know that after every game there will be parents and players who will blame the umpires for missing calls. Calls that each team would say were obviously wrong or at least that's how they viewed them. But umpiring is a tough job and none of those parents complaining about the bad job would ever volunteer to do it themselves. That being said, I am sure that after this game the same complaints were heard. And with any luck, maybe someone passed around a donations cup so we all could contribute to getting the man behind me a gift card to the Eyeglass Warehouse.

Anyway, after the walked-in run, you could feel the tension in the air and a game we once had total control over was now slowly slipping away. I could feel myself breathing faster and I could hear my heart pounding over the noise of the crowd. I took a deep breath to try and calm my nerves but it didn't help much. I was nervous now, as it was clear that the runner on third base could change the direction of the game. The frustrating part was that Billy wasn't really throwing badly. He was consistently hitting the outside edge of the plate, which *was* a strike, just not tonight. I could only hope that Billy kept the ball up near the strike zone and didn't start throwing balls into the dirt. I am a good catcher but every once in a while one will get by me. With a runner on third that could be costly.

Billy was back on the mound looking for some direction from me so I threw down a couple of signs indicating fastball, again. Billy nodded okay and then went into his short delivery, but what came at me was the slowest fastball I have ever seen. I could have run to the snack shack, downed a couple hotdogs, and still been back in time to catch this ball. This was without a doubt a pitch that a batter could only dream of getting served; it was the pepperoni on the pizza, the icing on the cake, it was a home run and all it needed was a fence to fly over. I was practically drooling as I watched this pitch come in and I wasn't even the one batting. I know that I would have unloaded on this ball: I would have waited for the right moment and then launched it into outer space (well, at least the parking lot). But the key here was to be patient and wait.

Every sport has its equivalent of this pitch -- in soccer it's the breakaway, in tennis it's the easy volley, in golf it's the one foot putt, in football it's the open field catch and basketball has the wide open lay up -- and in every single sport there is also the choke. It's the moment of anticipation before the play where you get over-anxious and shank the putt, drop the catch and swat the ball into the net.

So it shouldn't have surprised anyone when the lucky batter's eyes grew large and he went for the pitch with everything he could muster up, only to be so far in front of the ball that he hit a dinger off the tip of his bat, directly towards the pitcher. The ball hit the dirt five feet in front of Billy, bouncing right into his glove. He relayed the ball right back to me at home plate for out number two, and I in turn gunned the ball to Marcus Neely, our first baseman, to try for the final out. It was the easiest throw ever, just 90 feet, 27,432 millimeters, 1,080 inches and .017 miles. I know what you're thinking, how did the slow kid remember all those numbers. It has to do with baseball, that's all I'm going to say. But I have been throwing all my life and have never had an easier throw. I once went to the county fair and spent an hour at the dunk tank knocking Chief Sterlin into the water. I put him in a record 30 times on 32 throws, so I don't have to tell you that I could hit a hit a bull's-eye in the middle of a tornado. But at this moment, with the wind silent and calm, all I could do was watch in horror as my throw went sailing over Marcus's head and into right field. By the time we recovered the ball two runs had scored and the game was over.

"Stephen," Miss Stanton called out.

"Yes, Ma'am?"

"In what year did Lewis and Clark start their expedition to the west and on what river did they travel?"

"Year?" I asked, trying to buy myself some time.

"Yes, Stephen. What was the year and what was the river?"

I closed my eyes and tried to think. I knew that all eyes were on me now. I guess this was the teacher's way of punishing me for not paying attention, but it was a mean way to do it. I didn't need anyone's help embarrassing me in front of my peers. I did that very well all on my own.

Then suddenly I heard a whisper from behind me say, "1804 on the Mississippi."

I opened my eyes and looked at the teacher and hesitated. My first inclination was to spew out the answer I'd just heard, but then I thought, what if someone is messing with me. What if they gave me the wrong answer to try and make me look stupid? It would be just like one of the bully gang to try and make me look bad. They've done it before. But then I thought, what's the difference? I didn't know the answer anyway, so whatever answer I came up with on my own was going to be wrong.

"1804 and they traveled the Mississippi," I blurted out.

"Correct! Very good." Miss Stanton sounded as puzzled as she looked but moved on. "Can anyone else tell me how long their journey lasted?" Hands shot in the air, not mine of course. "Yes,

Megan."

"It took them over two years, from May 1804 to September 1806."

"Very nice, Megan," Miss Stanton praised her.

Megan Milton was the new girl in town and if I had to guess, also the little bird chirping answers in my ear. I didn't know much about her but I certainly appreciated her help. No one else in this class would have bothered. They would have been perfectly content just letting me sit there and sweat it out. As the teacher moved around the class calling for more answers, I again slipped away.

The sweat was dripping off of my face and the catcher's gear now felt like it weighed a thousand pounds. I could hear gasps from the crowd and then the sound of cheers. I could see and feel the disappointment flooding over my teammates. The tears welled up in their eyes, but I would never cry. I lost the game. It was my fault and I would certainly take full responsibility for my mistake. But if it weren't for that last throw I would have played a perfect game. I had five hits and scored three times and I threw out two runners at second and one at third. I had a great game and no one could take that away from me. Unfortunately what everyone else will remember is that awful throw to first base and the loss of the game.

"Stephen," I heard the coach call out. "Come here."

I walked toward the coach looking at the ground the whole way. I was feeling sorry for myself but mostly embarrassed. I couldn't even imagine what he was going to say about that throw. When I got close enough to talk to him I could feel the emotions welling up inside me and I had to fight it back. “Don’t you dare cry,” I told myself.

“I am so sorry, Coach,” I said shaking my head still in disbelief. “I don’t know how that ball got away from me. I feel terrible.”

The coach put his hand on my neck and gave it a fatherly squeeze and said, “I know you do, I can see it. But try not to be too hard on yourself. There were a lot of reasons we lost this game and most of them had nothing to do with that throw.”

“But I should have gotten him.”

“We all made mistakes today, including me. That is part of the game and it’s part of being human. You can’t dwell on them. Learn from them and move on. Do you know what I mean?”

“I guess.”

“So, what did you learn?”

“I need to practice that throw.”

“No, Kid, you have a cannon for an arm! You threw out three base runners tonight. You can make that throw in your sleep. You let up is what you did. You saw the easy out in front of you and instead of throwing the ball with purpose you eased off the throw and the ball sailed away on you.”

“I choked!”

“Stephen, it happens and I’m sure in your baseball career it will likely happen again. Just don’t let it get in your head or it will get locked there, and if that happens you’ll start to make that same mistake over and over. So shake it off, kick some dirt, stomp your feet, shout about it if you like, but get it out of your system and forget about it.”

"It's easier said than done, Coach. I hate to lose."

The coach laughed. "Me too, but it is one loss and we have lots of time to get it back. Plus losing builds character, right?"

"I guess."

"Take my word for it, we will be a better team because of this game. I want you to go home tonight and get a good night's sleep and put this game behind you. We have the Cardinals tomorrow and they're a good team. And Stephen?"

"Yes, Coach?"

"If you decide to take my advice and start stomping and shouting, just don't do it here in front of everyone. It will make you look like a bad sport and we don't want that, do we?"

"No sir."

"Good. Now go get everyone together and meet me in left field so I can go over the game and get you guys out of here."

Despite what the coach had said, sleep didn't come easy after losing this game. I kept seeing that throw in my head over and over, wishing somehow I could get a do-over. Losing may very well build character like the coach said, but it still felt awful.

"Stephen!"

"Yes, Miss Stanton?" When I looked up she was standing right in front of my desk.

"You really need to pay attention. If you paid better attention then maybe you wouldn't get D's on your papers."

Of course she said this as she was putting last week's test down in front of me with a great big D written across the front. She even wrote a little note for me at the top that said, "Need to pay attention!"

in big red letters.

The kids in class began to laugh and I just wanted to go someplace and hide. The dismissal bell rang in the nick of time and everyone shot out the door. But even with no one else there, my knees were shaking when I stood up, like a boxer who just got knocked to the ropes and couldn't stay up. I walked down the hall in a daze, lost in another moment of embarrassment.

Chapter 7

The New Girl

The school bell rang on and off throughout the day. It rang to let us know it was time to change classes or to tell us lunch was over. It was like a traffic light that kept the traffic flowing. But that last bell was a special one and it was usually my favorite, except today. Today it was muffled with the sound of kids laughing at me and the sight of another D.

As I walked through the double doors of the school leading to the buses, I heard a girl's voice say from behind me,

"That was just mean."

Still a little out of sorts and distracted, I turned slightly and saw that it was the new girl, Megan. She was talking to me. I didn't think she was at first but she was looking right at me so I said,

"What?"

"I said, that was mean. It was a mean thing to do. And she shouldn't be doing it in front of the whole class."

I really didn't know what to say so I just said, "I guess."

"You guess?"

"She just wants me to pay attention."

"That may be true but she also picks on you. I don't see her doing that with anyone else."

"You think she picks on me?" I asked, kind of surprised that she seemed to care.

"Do I think?" she said sarcastically. "Yeah, I think. She picks on you and I think she likes it too."

"You do?"

"Yes, I do," she said and rolled her eyes. "Don't you?"

"Yeah, it does seem that way sometimes."

"Well you know what, she has no right ..."

I quickly found out that Megan likes to talk. And the more she talked about Miss Stanton the more worked up she was getting over it, and the more worked up she got the quicker she talked. It was like someone emptied a bucket of balls into a pitching machine and couldn't turn it off. The words were coming at me faster than I could swing and my brain hit overload, getting foggy.

When this sort of thing comes on and my head fogs over, the sounds of the world disappear. It's like the constant rush of a freeway. After a while it becomes what they call white noise and you don't hear it anymore. Megan's voice was now becoming white noise and it wasn't long before I found myself staring at her, simply nodding. Most of the time when this happens to me I am sitting in class where I disappear into thoughts about baseball, but not this time.

Right now I was looking at this girl and I just started to notice things about her that I found appealing. Like the way she smiled. It was a little crooked, and her teeth were shiny white. They weren't perfectly straight but they weren't all scattered about her mouth either. It was her front two teeth that caught my attention because they crossed each other just a little at the bottom. I like it. I don't know why but something about it made her more interesting to look at. I know this might sound weird but I was really enjoying just looking at her. She has the greenest eyes I have ever seen. Actually, as I think about it, I don't think I have ever seen anyone with green eyes before her. But they are so cool.

I think the fact that I found her eyes so fascinating and I kept looking at her helped it seem like I was listening because she just kept talking. As she continued I watched her expression change many times. One second she'd smile and then get serious and then laugh. Then she'd get serious again, smile and then laugh. She had one of those contagious laughs too. And even though I didn't hear a word she said, when she started to laugh I could actually feel myself smiling. I was watching and hearing her laugh, enjoying every second of it. Then it dawned on me that what I was experiencing was a bit odd even for me, so I thought maybe it was time to come back to the real world. I had the ability to shake myself back to reality if I had to. But just as I was thinking this, she reached up and pulled a red stretchy band out of her hair and all the hair that had been pulled off of her face came down. It didn't look that long when it was up, but it was pretty long and when it fell, it all seemed to happen in slow motion, like a shampoo commercial. Her hair landed in the middle of her back and on her shoulders with these curls bouncing around like stretched out springs. The color is a mix of light browns and blonds. It's beautiful. *She* is beautiful.

I can't believe I am standing here thinking this stuff about another person, but it's true. Then suddenly, out of nowhere, I actually heard her words.

"... don't you think? Don't you think?"

She sounded concerned and her words pulled me out of my fog, bringing me back to the moment. I hesitated for a second without answering her and then, because I had no idea what to say, I blurted out, "I'm not sure."

She looked at me like maybe I was crazy. "You don't think you should stop the bus? How are you going to get home if you let the bus leave without you?"

"What?"

"Your bus, it's leaving without you."

"Oh, that's okay. I always walk home when the weather is nice." It wasn't true, but I thought it sounded better than me saying daaaa and then have her watch me chase after the bus.

"Wow, that's cool, but I have to catch mine. See you tomorrow."

"Oh, okay. See you tomorrow," I said.

I watched her run to the bus and climb up the stairs, the folding doors closing behind her. My eyes followed her right up to the point where she sat down. Then, as the bus pulled away, I could see her wave at me and smile. That cool, crooked smile. That smile that was now locked in my head even though she was gone.

I had never actually walked home from school before, probably because it was insane to walk the four miles when you can jump on a bus. But today at least I would have company all the way home.

Megan Martin, the girl with the slightly crooked teeth and beautiful eyes; I just could not get her out of my mind.

Chapter 8

Jack

It only took me an hour to get home. I walked a little and ran a little; all in all it wasn't so bad. And I made it back long before my parents got home from work. My mom works as an office manager in a small law firm about twenty minutes away so she is one of the few moms in Lamington that does go to work each day. I wasn't sure if she'd like the idea of me walking home today, but with Jack around there were rarely any secrets. By day's end I would most likely know her feelings on this issue.

Jack was in the kitchen when I walked in the back door and didn't waste a second before hitting me with questions.

"What happened to you?"

"What do you mean?" I asked.

"You weren't on the bus!"

"Yeah, I know. It was a nice day so I decided to walk home."

"You never do that."

"Well I did today."

"That's a long walk. Why would you do that?"

"Because I felt like it."

"I would never walk all that way, it's crazy."

"It's not crazy, you're just lazy," I said, laughing.

"No I'm not, I just wouldn't do it."

"That is why you are not me."

"No one in their right mind would choose to walk that far, that's why we have buses."

"Well no one cares what you think," I said.

"So are you going to tell me who the girl was?"

"What girl?"

"The girl you missed the bus for? I saw you talking to her."

"I told you I just decided to walk home."

"Sure you did. So who was the girl you *didn't* miss the bus for?"

"None of your business."

"What's the big deal, who is she?"

"Don't you have someplace to be?"

"No, so who is she?"

"You don't know her."

"I know I don't know her, that is why I asked you who she is."

"She's in my last two classes if you really have to know."

"What's her name?"

"Megan."

"Where does she live?"

"What's with all the questions? I don't know where she lives. Don't you have to practice the trombone?"

"I did that while you were walking. So why haven't I ever seen her before, is she new?"

"So everybody you've never seen before has to be new?"

"No, but she's pretty. I just think I would have noticed her before, that's all."

"Well, she is new, so that is why you have never noticed her."

"So what is she doing talking to you, taking pity on you?"

"Listen Four Eyes, you better watch the pity talk or next time the Sullivan brothers are pushing you around I could just look the other way. You might be way smarter than me but you don't see those kids in my face, do you? I've got your back Little Brother so you better have mine."

"Sorry, I didn't mean anything by it."

"Yeah, sure you didn't."

"Really, I was just kidding."

"Hey, it is what it is. You're smart and I'm not. I will have to learn to live with that just like you have to live with the forty-one times you struck out last season."

"It was actually fifty-six if you count the playoff games. If you're going to quote my statistics at least get them right. I had fifty-six strikeouts, but two walks and I was hit by five pitches so at least I got on base seven times," Jack said proudly.

"Yeah, but how many times did you get picked off at first?"

"Six."

"So if you think about it you really only got on base once all season." I looked at him and smiled.

"Ha, ha, ha."

"Well at least you only have three strikeouts so far this

season."

"We've only played one game."

"Well then think about it this way, maybe you'll break last year's record. I don't think that anyone has ever struck out every single time that they've batted. I could be wrong, but it sounds like an achievable goal."

"Gee, that's a record I want to hold," he said sarcastically.

"Listen to me, and I'm being serious here. Just lay off the high fastballs. If you do that then you might even walk more than you strikeout this year."

"Yeah, I know, I'll try. I just want to get a hit."

"I know, we all have our dreams. I would like to get straight A's."

"Maybe we should both start with smaller goals," Jack said, and then we both busted out laughing.

I knew he would never lay off the high fastballs. For some reason he was drawn to that pitch like a moth to a lightbulb. The bad thing for him is every pitcher in the league knows it so it's almost the only pitch he ever sees.

In sports there is never a sure thing and you can never count your outs before you get them, but when Jack comes to bat, he is about as sure an out as you get.

Chapter 9

Locker Trouble

There is one thing that is for certain: there were never two people more different than Jack and I. We are brothers, and twins at that (with me being older by ten minutes), but we are as different as night and day. I have always felt that if we could have just been identical then maybe things would be different. Maybe then we would have more in common. But we're not and that unique bond that most twins share with each other just isn't there. In fact, we usually take very little interest in what the other one is doing. We just don't have a lot in common and the list of things that separates us grows by the year.

One thing that irritates Jack is that I am athletic and he's not. Also, I take after my dad's side of the family, with chiseled features and high cheekbones, plus I'm tall. Not one of Dad's four brothers is less than six feet tall and they are all strong solid guys. Just throw some flannel shirts on them, hand them axes and you've got Paul Bunyan and his brothers. Jack, on the other hand, takes after my mom. Not that this is a bad thing. My mom is a pretty woman with delicate features, chestnut-colored hair and she's on the small side. My dad says if she were a fish he would have to throw her back. But when I stand next to her she comes up just a little under my chin so I think dad is over-exaggerating a bit. Jack, though, has to be three or four inches shorter than her, so he's not growing very fast. Jack is also bony, awkward, clumsy and annoying (and the last one he gets from my mom's brother because he is exactly the same way). Jack did inherit my mom's perfect hair, right down to the color, so he's got me there. Mine is all wavy and hard to manage where he can run a comb through his and be ready to go in a minute. Jack also got all the smarts and don't think for a second that I wouldn't like a little bit of that to be thrown my way.

Jack's a smart kid. I have to give him that, and he spends a lot of his time trying to get smarter. You will usually find him doing something on his computer or with his nose buried in books, where I will be out playing sports or riding my bike. Jack has a few friends and made even more when he took up the trombone a few years ago. If Jack isn't studying then he is usually hanging out with his trombone-playing friends from the school band.

The funny thing about Jack and the trombone is that they are a perfect fit. He couldn't have picked an instrument that fits his personality more precisely: they are both loud and grate on the nerves, and neither one seems to be growing on me. The truth is he loves the trombone every bit as much as I love baseball, which wouldn't be bad if he'd only play while I was getting gassed in the dentist chair. At least if I had the gas to numb the pain it would be a better experience. The dentist calls it laughing gas, though I'm not sure why, because it has never made me laugh. It just makes me woozy, which is a perfectly good condition to be in for Jack's trombone practicing. I think there should be a law that forbids all wind instruments from being practiced at home until you get good at it; for school use only.

School is one place that I don't see much of Jack. He is in all of the advanced classes so we rarely cross paths. Occasionally I will see him having lunch or find him in a hallway getting pushed around by the Sullivan boys but that's about it. Jack is a nice target for bullies too because he is small and kind of goofy. But most kids who like to bully know he's my brother and stay far away from him. The Sullivan brothers are another story though. They seem to have a very short memory, probably due to eating lead paint or being dropped on their heads a lot as babies. But whatever the reason, their convenient loss of memory where Jack is concerned is both irritating and troubling.

At six foot two and two hundred pounds I can be a bit intimidating to most kids. But to the Sullivans, it just doesn't seem to faze them the littlest bit, and that has always baffled me. I just can't understand how they could see me coming and pretend like whatever they're doing isn't a big deal. The last time I had to deal with them is a good example.

"Shane, what do you think you're doing?" I said.

"Helping your brother look for his coat," Shane said while laughing.

"So by shoving him inside his locker you think that you're helping him?"

"Stephen, he asked for our help," Dwayne chimed in, trying to hide his amusement.

"Dwayne, I think you should stay out of this. Your brother has enough problems at the moment without having to worry about you. Or are you telling me that you were helping too?"

"No, no, NO, I didn't say that."

"Good, then get out of here!"

That was all I needed to say and Dwayne disappeared like he had suddenly gotten sucked up by a twister.

"Look at him go, Shane. I don't think I have ever seen anyone run so fast. Now it's just you and me."

"Listen, I told you I was just helping him and that is all I was doing."

"Jack, are you okay?" I asked.

"Been better," Jack replied.

"Shane, it doesn't sound to me like Jack appreciates all the help you are giving him, does it?"

Shane didn't say anything, but it was one of those questions that wasn't supposed to be answered anyway. There's a name for it but I can't remember what it is. I know it starts with an R. Retotical? Rhetorical? Yeah, something like that.

"Jack, what do you think, do you appreciate Shane's help?" I asked.

"Not really," Jack's voice echoed from inside his locker.

"Shane, Shane, Shane," I said, shaking my head, "I think we have a problem here."

"Listen, if you touch me I am going to tell, then you'll get suspended and they will kick you off the baseball team." Shane took a step back.

"Shane, look at me and make sure you pay attention. Do I look like I care?"

"No, but you should."

"But I don't!"

"But you should!"

"But I don't, and that is a big problem for you this time, Shane. I am not going to keep going over this with you. I am done asking you to stop. That is my brother you've stuffed into that locker and it's not okay. You're hurting him, and if you are hurting him then you are hurting me. If someone were trying to hurt you what would you do?"

"I don't know."

"Shane, come on, what would you do?"

"Fight back I guess."

"You guess?"

"I would fight back, okay, that's what I would do."

"Exactly, so we do understand each other!" As I said this I took my backpack off of my shoulder and set it on the floor.

"But you'll get kicked off the baseball team," Shane said again, but this time it sounded flat and desperate.

It was at that moment that I understood Shane's thinking. I don't know why I didn't see it before but in Shane's mind this was his trump card, this was his magical hold over me -- baseball -- and once that string snapped he had nothing left and he knew it.

I just looked at him, smiled and shrugged my shoulders, like *oh well.* You could see his jaw drop open as the reality of his situation suddenly sunk in. His face went as white as a hotel bed sheet and he was looking around in a panic hoping that someone was going to swoop in and save him. He was like a lion hunter who had his prey cornered only to discover he was out of bullets.

For the first time you could see fear in his eyes. Probably the same look my poor brother had every time he was bullied by them. Then, before I could say another word, Shane was gone. He was gone so fast you could almost feel the breeze he left behind blow your hair back.

I never planned on laying a hand on him. I really didn't. I honestly didn't think I would have to. But don't think for a second that if I had to choose between my brother's safety and baseball that I wouldn't put my brother first. We may have our differences and at times we might not even like each other, but he is still my brother. I would never stand by and watch someone hurt him. Never.

Jack has been bully-free now for nearly two months. And in that time the only part of either of the Sullivan brothers that I have seen has been their backsides as they take flight around corners or through doors, most likely hiding from me.

My dad says that fear is a good equalizer. That it keeps people honest and on the right side of the line. But it isn't the way I want people to perceive me. I'm a nice guy and that is who I want to be. My dad also says that violence never has a good outcome and even the well-meaning get themselves hurt or even killed if they turn to violence. He says that it should only be used as a last resort, in dire situations.

I know when he says this kind of stuff he is usually talking about the problems that our government gets our country into but I think it applies elsewhere too. In his strange way I am sure he is trying to teach me a life lesson. Hey, look, I remember something! Maybe there is hope for me yet. Violence bad, diplomacy good.

Chapter 10

Diplomacy

Giants vs. Cardinals

I guess when Devlin Bellhouse's first pitch of my very first at bat against the Cardinals came crashing into the back of my helmet I should have just gotten up off the ground, brushed myself off, taken a deep breath and thanked my lucky stars that I didn't end up in the hospital. Diplomacy, right? No violence. But I couldn't help but wonder if it was a pitch that got away from him or it was intentional. It is pretty well known that Devlin doesn't like me. He is one of the popular kids at school and as far as he is concerned, he is the shining star and I am stealing his light.

Devlin is a great all-around athlete; there is nothing he can't do well and everyone, especially Devlin, thinks that he is bound for greatness. You would think being this talented would be enough for anyone, but not for Devlin.

Devlin doesn't like the competition so, in his mind, the best way to get rid of me is to find ways to chip away at my self-esteem and my confidence. And at school he has plenty of friends to help him do this, both boys and girls. At school these kids (aka the bully gang) ignore me like I'm not there, they shun me, or sometimes they invite me to things that aren't happening. They have had parties inviting everyone in our grade and intentionally leave me off the list. I have gotten anonymous notes with demeaning comments in them or I'll hear random name-calling when I can't see who is speaking. I even started to receive things in the mail, like subscriptions to magazines and music CDs. Of course these items weren't meant as gifts, they were sending a message, like the collection of Liberace CDs. My first thought was, Liberace? Who is he and why would I be getting these? I didn't know. I came to find out that he was a gay entertainer who is dead now but he sang and played the piano in Las Vegas. Ha, ha, I get it, how funny were they; it was their creative way of calling me gay. Very funny.

Physically, Devlin and his friends can't take me on because I am bigger and stronger than all of them. Even though Devlin is nearly the same height as me, I have him in weight by at least forty pounds. That makes physically challenging me less appealing so it became a game of mental bullying. None of them actually wants to get hurt trying to battle me. Some of them don't even want me to know that they are a part of Devlin's little group -- there is security in anonymity, like spies. But with all this going on, the one place that I am untouchable is on the ball field. It is just him and me and he wouldn't dare do or say anything without help.

So I had no doubt that Devlin hitting me with this pitch was his way to scare me, to intimidate me or maybe to even get me tossed from the game. As I took my first step in the direction of the pitcher's mound it was that thought that stopped me. I couldn't let him beat me. I couldn't let him into the only place in the world that makes me really happy and take that joy away. So instead of going after him, I stopped myself and jogged to first base knowing in my mind that I did the right thing. Plus, I knew there were other ways to make him pay and I would just take advantage of my free pass.

My ears were still ringing from how hard the ball hit my helmet, but my mind was never clearer. If he wanted to get me out he was going to have to earn it, and I was going to make him work for it, that was for sure.

Devlin was an overpowering pitcher for some of the kids on my team and I knew there was a good chance I could get left stranded on base, but it was my goal to step on home plate. I took a short lead at first and he made it a point to throw over or look me back several times before he ever delivered a pitch to the next batter. Devlin had a great move to first so stealing on him was hard; not many could do it, but it could be done. I don't know how other base runners steal but I like to concentrate on the pitcher's lower body. I watch the legs and the feet and just wait, wait, wait and then as soon as the pitcher's foot hits the point where he has no choice but to throw to the catcher, I RUN! *NOW!* I screamed in my head and you could see the dirt come flying off of my cleats and I could hear the infield yell,

"He's going, he's going!"

The adrenalin kicked in and my heart was slamming into my chest. I could see the second baseman preparing to make the catch so I knew the ball was coming. He caught it high and to the right of the bag so I went left, just narrowly beating the tag.

"Safe!" the umpire called out.

I kept a poker face but I had a celebration going on in my head. I brushed myself off and never gave Devlin even a glance. He quickly called time out and the whole infield went to the mound for a powwow. They were all huddled around Devlin with their gloves over their mouths. I was sure with no outs and me now on second base, it was giving him something to think about. If it were anyone else he would just battle it out with the batter. But it was me and I knew it would kill him to let me score.

The problem for him now is I was in his head. He had lost track of the big picture, which was the game at hand, and this was affecting his pitching. Will stood at the plate and watched the first two pitches sail high for balls. I decided to pull back and give Devlin the next three pitches. I wanted him to relax a bit; he was expecting me to run so he was looking for it. He looked back at me a few times and both the second basemen and shortstop kicked dirt and made noise behind me. But I wasn't going anywhere and I didn't give them any reason to think I was.

Devlin threw his first strike to Will on the fourth pitch but then walked him on the fifth. This left Devlin talking to himself, though I couldn't hear what he was saying.

"Ball four! Take your base," the umpire said.

I was now really enjoying this as I watched and waited and waited and waited and then, just as the catcher started to release his throw back to the pitcher, NOW, I screamed to myself. RUN, NOW! And I was off to third with my feet moving in desperate long strides. This was a bold move and one my coaches were not going to like, especially if I got thrown out. But I was like a bullet heading to the target.

The usual panicked screaming from the infield began, which took Devlin by surprise. The catcher tried to stop his throw and switch directions but couldn't. Instead he made an awkward throw to the pitcher and by the time the ball got to third I was already starting to pop up out of my slide. All of a sudden there was more screaming from the infielders as Will, not missing a beat, stepped on first base and then just continued to run. With everyone screaming at the third baseman to throw to second, no one could hear Devlin on the mound. He was screaming too, but no one heard what he was trying to say.

Baseball is a game of strategies, kind of like chess, and you have to think ahead three or four moves. As the king chess player, I knew exactly what Devlin was saying, the same thing that I would have said -- hold the ball.

But the third baseman took the bait and went for Will. As soon as he did I was on my way home. And if you thought the screaming was loud before, it was now deafening as they saw me going for home. There wasn't a coach, a player or fan that wasn't adding to the volume. I was told later that people heard the game all the way in the next town. Everyone jumped up to their feet screaming, and I mean everyone. It was so loud that when the ball was relayed back to the catcher from second you couldn't hear the umpire's call. But his signal was crystal clear. There were the expected groans from one side and cheers from the other. I got up, brushed myself off and stood at home plate long enough to watch the number 1 flicker onto the scoreboard under the runs column. I looked over at my dad who was smiling and clapping and I heard his voice in my head say, "Diplomacy 1, Violence 0."

Devlin pulled himself together and went on to pitch a great game. I got two singles off of him but was unable to score again. I pressed him on the base path throughout the game and stole second two more times, but the Cardinals weren't going to make the same mistakes twice. Devlin just plowed through the rest of our lineup, leaving me stranded both times. My brother Jack, who also plays for the Giants, played right field, but not more than the minimum number of innings required by the little league board. He struck out swinging three times at pitches way over his head. He did play right field successfully since no balls were hit in his direction, thank you Baseball Gods. When the last pitch was thrown and the dirt settled the score was still Giants 1, Cardinals 0.

Chapter 11

Bad Sports

Devlin walked into his bedroom and whipped his baseball glove down on his bed. "I should have won that game," he said angrily.

Kevin, who was Devlin's best friend and also the Cardinals' left fielder, followed Devlin into his room and said, "It's all Jimmy's fault. Why in the world didn't he hold onto the ball?"

"Because no one thinks on this team but me! I am screaming at him to hold the ball and the rest of our team is calling for the throw. I even got out of the inning after that. Stephen's brother could have played third base better than that. Maybe we should ask the coach to trade for him," Devlin said sarcastically.

"That might not be such a good trade," Kevin said.

"I am just making a point, I know he's awful. Do you remember last year when that fly ball went off the front of his head?" Devlin said, laughing.

"I know, one second his glove was up waiting to catch the ball and then THUMP." Kevin laughed, falling onto Devlin's bed. "The ball even bounced about five feet into the air."

"He went down like a sack of potatoes. I would be embarrassed if my brother played like that."

"Me too," said Kevin.

"That Lurch Stephen doesn't seem to be bothered by it."

"Well he should be."

"Stephen doesn't seem to be bothered by anything."

"I know," Kevin agreed.

"I guess that's what happens when you're born dumb."

"That's probably why that pitch you bounced off his head didn't affect him, you can't hurt stupid people."

"Exactly."

"I thought you had him though."

"Me too. I thought when he stepped towards me that he was coming."

"I did too," agreed Kevin, "but you do know he might have gotten a couple of punches in before we could have saved you."

"It would have been worth it to see him get thrown out of the game."

"Now what? What's the plan?" asked Kevin.

"I don't know, nothing seems to be working."

"I know if I were him I would be ready to crawl into a hole and never come out."

"I can't believe the Liberace CDs didn't push him over the edge," Devlin said.

"Maybe we should buy some gay magazines and put them in his backpack," Kevin suggested.

"Yeah, and who's buying those? Not me. What if we got caught with them before we had a chance to get them in his bag? How would we explain them?"

"You've got a point. So what then?"

"I don't know. I want to do something big."

"Like what?" Kevin said.

"I want to get him kicked off the baseball team. That's what I want to do," Devlin said firmly.

"How?"

"I don't know, that's the problem."

"Think. What could he do that is so bad they would take him off the team?"

"Cheat," said Devlin with a smile.

"Cheat," Kevin echoed.

"Yeah, cheat!"

"How do we make someone look like they are cheating at baseball?"

"We don't," said Devlin knowingly.

"Then what?" Kevin asked curiously.

"School, that's what."

"But how are we going to make it look like he cheated in school? He is so stupid that no one will believe it."

"He is always struggling and that's why they will believe it," said Devlin.

"You think?"

"I do, and I think we can get Miss Stanton to do the job for us."

"How's that?" Kevin asked.

"You see the way Miss Stanton treats him."

"Yes."

"She's always bothering him."

"So?"

"So she is going to help us," said Devlin.

"She is never going to do that."

"Not knowingly."

"Then how?" Kevin asked.

"Here's what we have to do, and you need to make sure you do everything that I tell you to do because we can't have this come bouncing back to us."

"Okay, what?"

"We need that little freak Jeffrey to help us again, but you need to make sure that he thinks it is all his idea so he will want to do all the work."

"Do you think he will do it? Helping Deidre and Jenni with notes and mailings is one thing, but you're talking about him getting Stephen into big trouble."

"He'll do it. Jeffrey wants in with us so bad I think he will do almost anything to prove he's cool."

"Devlin, I don't want him hanging with us."

"He won't be, we just need to lead him on a little. We'll blow him off once he's done."

"Wow, that's cold."

"I know," Devlin said laughing.

"So what's the plan?"

Chapter 12

Charlie Time

Do you have any friends who have been around so long you can't really remember ever not having them in your life? For me, that's Charlie. I can't actually tell you how we met or what we did the first time we played together, but I have no memories of life before Charlie. I know we moved to Lamington from Utica, New York but I was just a baby. I know that my dad moved us here for a teaching job because he couldn't find work in Utica, and I know my parents and his parents became friends and that is how we all met. But these are not memories of mine. These are stories told to me by people who have those memories. But now, after ten years of living here, I have lots of my own memories of our time together. We've been through good and bad times and, like friends do, we share our hopes and dreams.

Now just because you are friends with someone doesn't mean they can't also be a pain. Charlie can sometimes drive me nuts. He's a joker and a bit on the sarcastic side so trying to get a straight answer out of him is often a hard thing to do.

The rumor floating around school today is that the Cardinals got

robbed and would have won if it weren't for some bad calls, with the worst and most obvious one being the call at home plate. According to everyone I was out by a mile.

"Did you hear the rumor?" I asked Charlie.

"What? I missed that, what did you ask?" said Charlie.

"Did you hear that rumor?" I asked again.

"Did I hear what?"

"The *rumor*."

"Which rumor was that?"

"The one about me being out at home plate by a mile. I wonder who started that rumor."

"Oh that one."

"Yeah, that one. So you did hear it," I said.

"Of course I did, I'm the one who started it."

Charlie's a funny guy and I couldn't help but laugh.

"Yeah, right," I replied.

"Listen, someone has to keep you grounded or your head will get so big we won't get you through a door."

"Stop it, did you hear people talking or not?"

"Of course I did and they're just talking garbage. I was at the game and the throw wasn't even close. You beat him, no one else, and Devlin just can stand it. Don't let them bother you."

"I'm not."

"It sounds to me like you are."

"I'm not, really."

"Okay, if you say so. Then it won't bother you if I tell you that they also say you run like a girl."

"They said that?"

"Yep, and they said that you have a rag arm too."

"Who said that?"

"I don't want to tell you because you're going to get mad and do something that you'll regret. I can see in your eyes that you're getting a little steamed."

"I am not."

"I see what I see and you are," said Charlie.

"I'm not steamed, I just want to know who said it." I guess I was getting a little worked up but I really wanted to know. "Charlie, really, who said it?"

"You promise you won't do anything extreme?"

"I promise."

"I don't know. You won't go punch them out or something, will you?"

"No. What do you mean 'them'? It was more than one person?"

"Stop. Do you promise?"

"Yes, I promise, now who?"

"Okay, it was Jessica."

"Jessica? Your sister Jessica? She's eight," I said, rolling my eyes.

"I know, but she knows her baseball. You should see her hit off the tee. She also said that my grandmother can beat you in a foot race and she's dead."

Charlie started laughing, which made me laugh too. Charlie had my back and if push came to shove he would be there for me if I needed him. But he knew that I would let what people were saying bring down my spirits so he always had a way of making me see that I needed to let things go. He would say, "Just let it roll off your shoulders, like rain off the roof, like a wheel off your foot." He was always trying to lighten the mood.

"Have you gotten anything good in the mail lately?" Charlie asked.

"No, not since the CDs."

"Did you at least listen to the CDs?"

"No, who listens to Liberace? Why, do want to borrow them?"

"Help no!"

Charlie likes to use the word "help" instead of, well, you know; the word you're not supposed to say. He said the real word once and his mom washed his mouth out with soap so now he just says help. It's not overly clever and I think it sounds dumb but he likes it.

Charlie continued, "You wouldn't catch me listening to that junk. I was just double checking to see if they saw something in you that I was missing."

"You're a funny guy and that is going to get you into trouble one day," I said.

"Nah, as long as you're around no one is gonna mess with me."

Charlie isn't a big guy, but he has to be at least five foot six, which is a few inches taller than my brother, and he's thicker and stronger too. He is easy to spot in the school's crowded hallways because his strawberry blond hair and pasty white skin make him stand out like a neon sign. He also has the tiniest blue eyes you have ever seen. Charlie doesn't seem to have many worries, he's smart and gets good grades (though he does work hard to get them), but there are two things I know Charlie will never have to worry about: skin cancer, because he never leaves the house without sunscreen, and other people messing with him, because I will always have his back.

"You better be careful because I just might get Jack out here to kick your butt," I joked.

"Right, when pigs fly."

"No really, I plan on holding you while he kicks it."

"Yeah, okay, that might get the job done," Charlie said laughing. "What's with your brother anyway? Why is he still playing baseball? You would think forty-one strikeouts in one season would be enough incentive to hang up the cleats. I think he could be doing more productive things with his time."

"Like what?" I asked

"Like taking more trombone lessons. We can hear him practice all the way over at my house and it doesn't sound any better than when he started two years ago."

"It was fifty-six," I said.

"Fifty-six what?"

"Strikeouts. Counting the playoffs it was fifty-six, and he said he won't quit until he gets a hit."

"Well that's not going to happen."

"You do realize that he has struck out almost the same number of times that Janet Wilkins has turned you down, and yet you keep asking her out. He wants to keep trying too."

"That may be true, but I can keep trying until I am old and gray but he can't play little league into his forties."

"I like that, that's funny! And you know what, it makes sense too because once Janet is so old that all of her teeth fall out, like my grandmother, she will be *so* ready to date you."

"So you agree, I have a chance with her?" Charlie said smiling.

"Yeah, I think you do, if you live that long."

"I'll start working out."

"That's a start, but you might want to change your diet too."

"Change my diet? Change it to what?"

"You might want to eat healthier things."

"Like what?" Charlie said.

"Chicken."

"I'm not a big fan of bird. I do like bacon cheeseburgers though."

"You can't eat those."

"I love them."

"I know you do, but they've got to go. Too much fat. They will clog your arteries."

"I can still eat barbecue potato chips, right?"

"Gone!"

"No!"

"Yep."

"Chocolate chip mint ice cream?"

"Gone."

"Snickerdoodles?"

"Nope."

"Movie popcorn?"

"History, only hot air popped."

Charlie frowned. "What else can I eat?" he asked.

"Carrots, peas, salad, broccoli …"

"Stop, stop, stop! Those are all vegetables."

"Yeah, but they are all good for you and they will increase your life span. Isn't that the point, to pick things that will give you more time to ask Janet out?"

"Yeah, but those are *vegetables*."

"Yeah, so what?"

"I don't eat vegetables."

"I thought you want to go out with Janet?"

"Not if it means I have to eat vegetables. I draw the line right there. If Janet thinks that I am going to eat vegetables for the next thirty years just to get to go out with her she's out of her mind. I am breaking it off right now."

"You're not going out with her so you can't actually break up with her," I pointed out.

"You're right, but I'm done with her as of today. I am done." Charlie seemed lost in thought for a second and then his face lit up big and bright.

"What's that look for?" I asked.

"I just got a better idea."

"What's that?"

"I'm going to ask Peggy Sloan out."

"Peggy Sloan, why her?"

"Have you ever seen her eat?"

"No, I can't say that I have ever paid attention to how she eats."

"Next time you are in the lunch room watch her. She eats double servings every day and the best part is she always leaves the vegetables. Now *that's* the girl for me."

"I will have to watch her and if what you say is true then she might be the girl you're looking for."

"There is no might about it, she's the one. There is no way that girl will ever expect me to eat vegetables."

"That's true. Wow, when you make sense, you really make sense."

"I'm out of here," Charlie said as he began to walk away.

"Where are you going?"

"I am going to ask Peggy out."

"Now?"

"Yes, now. It's only a matter of time before every guy in this school realizes that she doesn't eat vegetables. Once they put it together like we just did, she will have so many guys to choose from that she might not go out with me. I need to ask her now, before it's too late. I'll see you later."

Peggy Sloan is probably going to be one of those girls my mom calls the swan. It's the girl in school that nobody ever gave a second glance and then one day you find yourself flipping through fashion magazines and there she is, Peggy Sloan Supermodel. Maybe Charlie is getting in a little early but I can see it happening.

Peggy is thin and sort of plain, but between the braces, a bad hairdo and her jumbo glasses, it's hard to see her as anyone's dating choice right now. But the more I thought about Charlie and Peggy together, something about it seems right. I think Charlie might even be good for her because in all the years that I've been in school with Peggy, I don't think I have ever seen her crack a smile. My mom says that smiling is very important in life, that it actually makes people happier. And when you are happy you are healthier, so Charlie might just be good for her.

Chapter 13

The Stick Up

When I walked into the cafeteria ten minutes later I expected I would find Charlie hanging out with Peggy. But instead Charlie was nowhere to be found and Peggy was eating lunch in her usual spot alone. I stood at the door for a second and scanned the cafeteria. I was hoping I would see Megan and, since she's new, I figured she'd be sitting by herself too. But no Charlie, no Megan. Well, not until she popped up behind me and stuck her fingers into my back and said,

"This is a stick up! Give me your lunch money." Then she giggled.

I turned around to face her. "You're a dangerous little thing."

"You want to have lunch?" Megan asked.

"Lunch?" I said, sounding surprised.

"Yeah, lunch. You know, food?"

"I was planning on it."

"With me, silly!" Megan said smiling.

"Well, I was planning on eating alone."

"Really?"

"Really."

"Can you cancel those plans?"

"I don't know, it's kind of late notice."

"Really?" she said, sounding playfully annoyed.

"Okay, but you will have to treat."

"Why?"

"Some crazy girl stole my lunch money," I said, and then I smiled.

"Okay, I'm buying. What's good today?" she asked.

"All I can tell you is stay far away from the pizza, and the burgers. The burgers are like shoe leather, unless you like shoe leather."

"Not so much."

"The fish squares are good as long as you put lots of tartar sauce on them."

"I wish we could leave and go out for lunch," she said wishfully.

"We could."

"Oh yeah? How do we get there?" Megan said, sounding all serious.

"I will have my driver's license in a few years and then we can take my car."

"Cool, but what do we do *now*?"

"Fish squares with tartar sauce, doubles for me please, and make sure you get the fruit cups. I love the fruit cups."

"Hey! I said I'd treat but I didn't realize I would have to buy you doubles!" Megan objected.

"Two milks too, if you don't mind."

"Two?"

"I'm a growing boy. You don't think I got this way by eating lettuce leaves do you?"

"Well don't you think you are big enough already? Maybe it's time to cut it down to singles and add some lettuce to your diet."

"Oh no!" I said sounding concerned.

"Oh no what?"

"You're not one of those girls who is going to make me eat vegetables are you?"

"What's wrong with vegetables?"

"Nothing, I like vegetables." I smiled. "And at least I won't have to worry about my friend Charlie hitting on you."

"Why not?"

"He won't date any girl who eats vegetables."

"Really?"

"Yeah, really."

"His loss," she said with a big smile.

There it was again, that smile and the crooked teeth. I should probably pinch myself to make sure I am not really sitting in Miss Stanton's classroom. She is probably going over long division at this very moment and I have slipped into my normal classroom coma. Megan couldn't possibly want to hang out with me, or maybe she has joined in with Devlin's posse and this is their next big joke on me. Yeah, let's get the new girl to mess with his head.

"Can I ask you a question?" Megan was staring at me.

"Sure, what is it?" I asked.

"Where do you go?"

"What do you mean, where do I go?"

"I watch you in class and there are times when you look like you have disappeared from this planet."

"Is it that obvious?"

"Sometimes it is."

"Wow, I didn't realize that."

"So, where do you go?" she asked again.

"Baseball."

"Baseball? What do you mean, baseball?"

"It is like my mind goes backwards in time and I replay games in my head. I'll go over things that I could have done differently. It's my chance to take all the things we did wrong in a game and make them right."

"Really?"

"Yep. It's not the only thing I think about, but that's what happens most of the time. Like yesterday, when Miss Stanton called on me I was thinking about the game I had the night before. I was going over and over it, reliving it, watching myself make the same bad throw again and again."

"That's no fun," she said.

"No, that wasn't fun, but I go over the good stuff too."

"Well at least that's better than rehashing the bad."

"Do you like baseball?" I asked.

"Yeah, I do."

"Well you should come see me play. I'm pretty good."

"I just might do that."

"Well, you should."

"Well, maybe I will."

"I'll have them hold a ticket for you at the gate."

"They have tickets?"

"No, I just heard someone say that in a movie once and I thought it sounded good."

"Well it does."

There was that smile again.

"So I will have them hold a ticket for you."

"You do that."

* * *

"Stephen, Stephen, Stephen!" a voice calls out.

"What, what is it?" I answered as my brother's voice snapped me out of my fog.

"It's time for dinner. Mom wants you to come down now."

"I'll be right down."

"Now!"

"I said I'm coming, Dog Breath, so leave me alone!"

"What are you doing in there anyway?"

"Same thing I am always doing in here -- homework."

"How is that working out for you?"

"Go away."

"No, hurry up! I'm hungry and Mom won't start without you."

The fact of the matter is it wasn't going well. I just finished reading the same chapter for the fourth time and all I can remember is that Lewis and Clark were the first Americans to cross the western part of the country. There was something about the continental divide and the Louisiana Purchase; I don't know what exactly. Thomas Jefferson also had something to do with it all.

"Stephen!" called Mom. She sounded impatient.

"I'm coming, Mom!"

"Now, not tomorrow!"

Chapter 14

Family Time

Once Jack had summoned me back from la la land I could smell dinner in the air. I wasn't sure what it was but it sure smelled good. So good in fact that it made my stomach rumble and reminded me just how hungry I was. I wasted no more time at that point, taking the steps down two at a time. When I got to the kitchen my family was waiting with the table set and the food already dished out on plates. It was meatloaf night with mashed potatoes, gravy and peas.

I love my mom's cooking and her meatloaf is fantastic. She bakes it in the oven until it starts browning and then pulls it out long enough to paint the top red with tomato paste, and then cooks it some more. The result is both tender and juicy with a flavor that does a little dance on your tongue. And her mashed potatoes are like eating a buttery cloud, they're so creamy. My mom's love of butter keeps them off the low calorie side of the menu though. And then there are the baby peas. I am not a big fan of peas in general, but the baby ones are okay and as long as I have ketchup I can eat almost anything.

My mom can turn almost any food into a dinner for the gods, with the exception of her pork chops. Her fear of raw pork is legendary in the Miller family and, because of this, pork chops in our house have been declared a lethal weapon by my dad. One night he held one up by the bone and said,

"Look, they even have built in handles for easy striking."

This probably was not something he should have said to a woman who had been cooking for an hour because after his declaration my mom took the chop she was eating and threw it at him from across the table. She nailed him square in the middle of his forehead. Unfortunately for him the bone from the chop hit him in a way that cut his forehead deep enough that my mom had to take him to the hospital to get stitches.

I thought my dad was going to be furious by this but, as it turned out, he was actually thrilled. He said it was exactly what he needed to prove my mom was producing weapons. This was a huge victory for my dad but one he didn't rub in her face either. As a matter of fact, now that I think about it, since the assault with the deadly pork chop incident he hasn't mentioned her pork chops at all. That's odd. I will have to ask him why. But today there will be no threat of food-related injuries because meatloaf doesn't have any bones and mashed potatoes are nice and soft.

"What took you so long?" Mom asked as I sat down at the table.

"I was doing homework."

"How's it going?" Dad asked.

"It's going."

"Did you get your test back yet?" Mom asked.

"Not yet, tomorrow maybe." The truth was I got it back with a big fat D written on it. I hadn't planned on mentioning it unless they asked. Time for a new plan.

"How do you think you did?"

"I don't know, Dad, can't we just eat?" I really didn't want to talk about the test over dinner. I was hungry and just the thought of it was giving me a sour feeling in my stomach, and I didn't want to spoil my meatloaf and mashed potatoes.

"Okay, don't get snippy," Mom said.

"I'm sorry, I'm just hungry."

"Well, let's get started then. We were waiting on you," Dad said.

We all bowed our heads and my mom said grace. We didn't waste any time digging into the food after that, and then Dad apparently wanted to clear up a rumor.

"Stephen, Jack told me you have a girlfriend. Is this true?" Dad was smiling as he said this.

Mom quickly gave me a concerned look and repeated, "Is that true?"

"No, it's not true, I don't have a girlfriend. I was talking to a girl the other day, that's all."

Leave it to Jack to make this national news.

"He had lunch with her today. I saw them, and they were cozying up next to each other in the cafeteria," Jack said smugly.

Right then I wanted to reach out and give Jack a great big hug. After two hours of Lewis and Clark my mind just kept going over lunch with Megan again and again, to the point where I started to believe it was one fantastic dream. When I got called for dinner and found myself in my room I was actually disappointed because I thought for sure I had imagined it all. But Jack is my witness, he saw me having lunch with her. I had lunch with Megan Milton!

"Stephen, is that true?" Mom asked.

"I had lunch with a friend, Mom. She just happens to be a girl."

"I saw him kiss her," said Jack

"Stephen, you didn't!" Mom said, shocked.

"I didn't kiss her." I rolled my eyes at Jack.

"You did, I saw you." Jack was having fun with this.

"Mom, don't listen to him, I didn't kiss anyone."

"I bet you were thinking about it though, weren't you?" said Jack. He had this mocking sort of smile on his face.

"What are you, two years old, Jack?" I answered.

"Be honest, you were thinking about it."

"Jack, stop it now. This is not the way we behave at the dinner table," Mom said sternly.

"Yeah, remember Jack, there is no fun at the dinner table," my dad said, and we all started to laugh, even my mom.

My mom doesn't like any sort of commotion at the dinner table, so if we joke around too much she will try and pull us back to a calm state. So out of the blue one day my dad just said, "Kids, there is no fun at the dinner table." This of course made us laugh, and Mom gave Dad the evil eye, but it stuck and now when he says it even Mom will laugh, sometimes.

"So what's your new friend's name?" Mom asked.

"Megan," I said and smiled.

"That's a pretty name," Mom said.

"Where does she live?" asked Dad.

"I don't know. She's new at school and I haven't asked her that yet."

"He doesn't know anything about her; I went over this all with him already," Jack chimed in.

"Shut your pie hole, Jack," I said.

He can be so annoying.

"Well, for a girl you claim to be in love with, you don't know very much about her," continued Jack.

"I am not in love and I never said I was."

"You're in lu-uv," Jack said, all sing-songy.

"I am not."

"Are too!"

"Mom, tell him to quit it before I stuff him in a locker at school. Or even better, you're the perfect size to hang off the new coatrack hooks."

"You wouldn't."

"Keep it up and you'll find out," I dared him.

"You're in love!" Jack said one last time as he left the kitchen and ran up to his room. "Stephen's in love."

"Are you guys sure we're twins?" I asked my parents.

"We're sure," said Dad, throwing up his hands like he was giving up.

"How sure?"

"Pretty sure," Dad said. "Your mom had twins and they sent us home from the hospital with the two of you."

"But you're not positive," I persisted.

"As positive as one can be about these things."

"But there is room for error?"

My dad gave me this blank sort of look, then said, "We never had your DNA tested if that's what you want to know."

"So there is a chance that he is not my twin?"

"A *slight* chance, I guess."

"How slight?" I was getting excited at this point.

"Oh, Stephen, I don't know. Marginal." My dad was sounding annoyed.

"What does that equal in percentage?"

"I don't know, maybe point zero nine percent."

"So you really don't know."

"Stephen, there is less than a one percent chance that he is not your twin, but it doesn't matter. What is most convincing for this ridiculous discussion is that he looks just like your mom's sister."

"He does not," my mom declared.

Mom hadn't commented until now. I had almost forgotten she was still in the room.

"He does too. Put a long blond wig on him and he is your sister's twin, not Stephen's."

"You are just getting ridiculous now. Both of you stop talking," Mom said with that tone she gets when she is annoyed.

But I still had more to say. "Dad, do you know who Jack and I really look like?"

"No, who?"

"Arnold Schwarzenegger and Danny DeVito in that movie 'Twins'."

"It's funny you said that, because I was watching you two on the ball field the other day thinking the same thing myself," Dad said laughing.

"Will you two stop. Jack might hear you," Mom said. Her face looked like she was trying not to laugh.

"Well it's true, Honey."

"Don't you and Jack have practice?" Mom said as she looked at me. You could tell she was trying to change the subject.

Dad answered, "They do, and I'll take them. Do you need anything while I'm out?"

"No, just finish eating and go before you both drive me crazy."

"Okay, and I'm sorry, but he does look like your sister Shelia, spindly legs and all. Give the boy some big old boobs and your sister is living in our house." Dad was laughing again.

"Get out of here," Mom said.

"Next time your sister is here, I will throw a wig on Jack and you will see."

"GO, NOW!" Mom had definitely had enough of this conversation.

"Okay, but you know I'm right."

"NOW!"

"Okay, okay," Dad said as he got up from the table.

"BYE!" we both said as we walked out of the kitchen.

The boys in our neighborhood love my aunt Sheila because she looks a little like that movie star Sharon Stone when she was younger, but with some extra enhancements. If we had a pool my friends would never leave my house when she visits, especially Charlie. I can barely get him to leave now when she's visiting and she's wearing regular clothes. If she was in a swimsuit he would be permanently camped out here.

Chapter 15

What's Up With Peggy?

Having your best friend live right across the street is great; we never have to worry about how we are going to get to one another's house. We just pick up the phone and say, "Can you come out?"

"Did you bring your glove?" I said.

"Got it," answered Charlie.

"Ball too?"

"Got it. Do you want to throw here or at the park?"

"Here's good, just try to keep the ball out of Stamitts' yard. I hate when he comes out screaming. You would think his lawn is made of gold."

Old man Stamitts hates people in his yard and doesn't miss an opportunity to bite your head off if you dare step foot in it.

"I can't throw as well as you, so no promises."

"I did say *try.*"

"Yep, got it."

The park is just down the road but I prefer to throw in the street in front of our houses. It's not like there's a whole lot of traffic to worry about. Every once in a while we have to move to one side to let a car go by but that's no big deal. Plus no one ever parks on our street so the ball has plenty of room for clear sailing.

"I've got to warm up a little so stay close," Charlie said.

"Sure," I replied.

Charlie then went into a pitching windup and threw the ball at me as hard as he could.

"What are you doing? You said you needed to warm up," I said, getting a little nasty.

"I am warming up," he said laughing.

"Do that again and I'll show you what a real fastball looks like."

"I'm not afraid of you."

"No?" I said. "Are you sure?"

"I'm sure. If my sister is right, you have a rag arm anyway."

"You've got a lot riding on an eight year old."

"That's true," Charlie said, "but I trust her judgment."

"Okay, you asked for it," I said and then went into my windup.

"Whoa, whoa, you're not really going to throw the ball from that close, are you?"

"Yeah, I was."

"What, are you crazy? You could hurt me!"

"You just did it to me," I said, defending myself.

"So what, I throw like a girl. Your arm is like a weapon. *Big* difference."

Charlie loves baseball as much as I do and we're both huge Yankees fans. He plays little league, just like me, but in left field for the Braves, who we beat today 21 to 2. Charlie is probably as good a player as most of the other kids but he doesn't take the game too seriously. The nice thing about Charlie and me is we never fight. And there are never any hard feelings over baseball games won or lost. As a matter a fact, after the game today he came over to my house and we caught the end of the Yankees game on TV.

"Okay, I'll go easy on you," I said, "but you better pull it back a little."

"I was just goofing around."

"So what happened with Peggy?" I asked, changing the subject.

"Who?" Charlie said.

"Peggy, the love of your life, the no vegetables girl."

"Oh, Peggy. Yeah, it didn't work out."

"Why not, I thought it was the perfect match?"

"It was."

"So what changed?"

"Bad timing," he said.

"What do you mean by that?"

"I saw her having lunch so I walked up and said hello ..."

"You did, really?" I interrupted, sounding surprised. I didn't really think that he would ask her out. Charlie talks a good game, but he has no follow through.

"Sure I did, why do you seem so surprised?"

"No reason. So what happened after that?"

"Nothing."

"Something must have happened. You don't just say hello to somebody and get no response. She didn't blow you off, did she?

The vegetable girl just blew you off?"

"Oh no, she didn't blow me off. She smiled."

"She did? That's good, right?"

"Wrong!"

"When is a smile not good?"

"When you have braces and you've just finished lunch."

"What do you mean?" I was lost here.

"She had been eating pizza," Charlie explained.

"So, you like pizza."

"I do, but once you eat it it should be gone."

"I don't understand what you're saying. She ate pizza and ...? Where didn't it go?"

"It was all stuck in her braces, pieces of bread, sauce and cheese all hanging there. It was gross."

"So ask her out when she hasn't just been eating."

"I don't know. I was thinking I'd just wait until she gets the braces off."

"That's another way to go, but aren't you worried about the other guys in school snatching her up?"

"No, not really."

"So you're just giving up on her?"

"Yeah, I think it's best."

I shrugged. "So who's next?"

"I was thinking I'll just lay low for a while, give the girls time to miss me."

"Lay low? You've been watching too many crime shows."

"So how about you? Jack tells me you were hitting on the new

girl."

"I wasn't hitting on her."

"That's not what Jack said."

"And since when did you start listening to Jack?"

"Since he told me you were hitting on the new girl and you conveniently failed to mention it."

"I haven't seen you since you went chasing after Peggy Sloan."

"Why do you keep bringing her up? Are you trying to hurt my feelings?"

"Sorry, what was I thinking, I know this must be a tough time for you," I said with mock sympathy.

"I forgive you."

"Oh gee, thanks."

"So did you really walk all the way home?" Charlie said.

"Jack, right?"

"Who else? He gossips like my Aunt Ella."

We were both laughing when we heard Charlie's mom shout, "Charles Martin Brandle! Get in zhis house now!"

"Your mom sounds mad," I said, "what did you do?"

When Mrs. Brandle is just talking to you her accent is very cool; her speech is almost like listening to a song. But when she is yelling, it is downright scary. It's like you've been captured by Hitler's army in Germany and they are pointing their guns and screaming at you in this language you don't understand. I was watching "Saving Private Ryan" and they did that. It was frightening. And that's kind of what Mrs. Brandle sounds like mad. My suggestion is to just stay on her good side.

Charlie's dad, on the other hand, is a quiet man and pretty much seems to let Mrs. Brandle run the house. Charlie said his dad and mom met in Holland when his dad was serving in the army. When he came back to the United States she came with him. I've always thought Mrs. Brandle looks kind of like the Swiss Miss girl on the hot chocolate box. She has a sweet-looking face and long pretty blond hair but then, like out of nowhere, she can turn into one of those evil mermaids from that one "Pirates of the Caribbean" movie. Really, when she's mad, you'd swear she could eat you alive.

"I said now!" yelled Mrs. Brandle.

"What did you do?" I asked Charlie again.

"I don't know, but I'm sure I'm going to find out."

Without waiting for Charlie to go in, Mrs. Brandle said, "Ver is zat pack of gum zat vas zitting on zhe counter?"

"I'm chewing it," Charlie answered.

"Not zhe whole pack? Tell me you haven't chewed zhe whole pack!"

"No, just a few pieces."

"You need to come in now!"

"Mom," Charlie said in protest.

"I mean now, zis zecond, not vhen you veel like it!" Mrs. Brandle paused and looked at me. "Hi Stephen," she said kindly in her broken English.

The Swiss Miss girl was back.

"Hi Mrs. Brandle," I said.

"Great game zhe other day. You keep playing like zhat and

ve'll be coming to zee you play at Yankee Stadium von day."

"Thanks, Mrs. Brandle."

"You're velcome," she said. Then, turning back to Charlie, "You're still standing zhere? Why are you still standing zhere? Get in zis house right now and for heaven's zakes, don't vart."

"Don't what?" Charlie said, not understanding.

"Vart, don't vart," she repeated. Then, "Good night, Stephen,"

"Good night, Mrs. Brandle. Bye Charlie," I said.

Charlie walked away and I just stood there thinking, what was *that* about? Don't fart? Mrs. Brandle was from a different culture and their customs were sometimes odd but this was off the charts weird. There is so much I can tell you about her but for now just know that she is not someone you want to mess with. Where some people have guard dogs and alarms, Charlie has his mom. Burglars, beware.

Chapter 16

Scheming

Monday was a strange day at school, enjoyable right to the end. Devlin and his friends were so caught up with something they were working on that they didn't bother with me; not a nasty note or a mean word all day. This is the way every day should be and there's really no reason that it shouldn't. My thinking now is that Devlin and his friends need to have more projects to keep those idle hands and mouths busy.

Now I might normally have been worried seeing them all huddled in a group like that, but the fact that Jeffrey Talin was sitting with them could only mean that it had to do with school. I knew Devlin wouldn't be caught dead hanging out with Jeffrey unless he had to. And I am sure that every second in his company had to be painful time spent for Devlin. Jeffrey was one of the smarter kids in our grade, which probably ran in his family since his dad was some big time lawyer in New York City. Jeffrey was not one of the popular kids though and he was always struggling to fit in somewhere. I liked him well enough and even found him funny at times, but a lot of the kids made fun of him. They called him The Gerbil. This was because of his overbite and his perfectly chubby round face and belly. These kids were cruel and then Jeffrey made it worse by coming in one day with his hair shaved into a crew cut which really made his features stand out. His mom didn't help him either by dressing him like a little executive with a dress shirt, khakis and suspenders. Every Friday he even added a tie, which I think he thought was the perfect extra, like a bright red maraschino cherry on the top of an ice cream sundae.

I guess Jeffrey and I should have bonded like brothers since we had similar experiences going on. But Jeffrey didn't live near me and he didn't play baseball so outside of school I had little contact with him. Other than being in the same grade, I hardly knew him at all.

* * *

"Kevin, I've got to go to class," Devlin said as he stood up. "I'll see you all later."

"You want to shoot some hoops after school?" Kevin asked.

"It sounds good to me. You in, Jeffrey?"

"What time?" Jeffrey asked.

"Right after school," said Devlin.

"I'll let you know later, I have to ask my dad," said Jeffrey.

"All right, I will see you unless I don't," Devlin said and gave Kevin a knowing head nod as he left the cafeteria.

Kevin and Jeffrey now sat at the cafeteria table alone. Kevin knew that Devlin wanted Stephen kicked off the baseball team and he didn't really care what the reasons were. If Devlin didn't like him, that was good enough for Kevin.

"Jeffrey, are you sure you sent him those CDs?" Kevin asked.

"I'm sure," Jeffrey answered.

"Well, it doesn't seem to be bothering him. Maybe you should come up with something better."

"Better?" said Jeffrey. "Like what?"

"I don't know, you're the one with the brains. I believe you told me you had all of these great ideas."

"I do."

"So what are they then? I don't think you really have any. I bet I can come up with a few though. Actually, you know what I think would be really funny is if someone could get him thrown off his baseball team. Now that would be funny."

"I could do that," Jeffrey said.

"Stop, you could not," Kevin said, egging him on.

"No, I could."

"How would you do that?"

"I don't know, but I could do it. I just have to think about it."

"Stop! You can't get thrown off a baseball team unless you get caught cheating or something and there aren't a lot of ways to cheat at baseball."

"What if he did something really bad in school?"

"Like what?" asked Kevin. This is what he had hoped Jeffrey would say.

"We could pull a fire alarm and say we saw him do it," Jeffrey suggested.

"I don't think that will get him thrown off the team, and then we also risk getting caught pulling it. I wish he would just cheat on a test. I think that could get him thrown off the team."

"If he got caught cheating in school they might kick him off."

"I know, that's what I just said."

"Well, I think that would work."

"We only have three weeks of school left. What is there left for him to cheat on?"

"A test, like you said."

"A test," Kevin said, laughing. "With the teacher standing in the middle of class you're going to figure out a way for him to look like he's cheating? Good luck with that."

"There is a way, I just have to think of it," Jeffrey insisted.

"You know what, Jeffrey, you tried. You get brownie points for trying. But honestly, short of him copying a term paper or something, I can't see how Stephen can get himself kicked off the baseball team." Kevin started to stand up from the table and he could practically see the wheels rolling in Jeffrey's head. "I'll see you tomorrow."

"Bye," said Jeffrey, but then he grabbed Kevin by the shirt.

"Kevin! I think I know how do it!"

"Sure you do. I'll believe it when I see it. Let go, Jeffrey. I'll see you later."

Kevin pulled away from Jeffrey and walked out of the cafeteria without waiting to hear Jeffrey's idea. When Kevin turned down the hallway, Devlin was waiting.

"Do you think he is going to do it?" asked Devlin anxiously.

"The only thing I can say is I put the idea in his head," Kevin said.

"Subtly, I hope."

"Very."

"Do you think he caught it?"

"With both hands, dude. With both hands."

"The paper is due Thursday."

"Yeah, I know. Thursday."

"Stanton will have to read them, which will take her a few days, so with any luck she will finish them over the weekend and by next week, Stephen should be toast."

"French," said Kevin.

"Toast!" Devlin followed up with a fist bump and they both disappeared down the hall.

Chapter 17

Doing Nothing

I don't know why, but something about Devlin and Kevin and the bully gang all together with Jeffrey was bothering me. They had picked on Jeffrey something terrible over the years and it was gnawing at me that a teacher had thrown him into that group of wolves, even to do school work.

I don't want to get all dark and depressing here but, to be honest, I just don't understand grown ups sometimes. Can't they see what is going on? It's all right in front of them. It makes me want to scream! It is so obvious, or maybe that's only because it is happening to me, to Jack, to Jeffrey, maybe to you. Is it possible that only if you experience being bullied it seems so clear? I am not going to lie to you, even though I go along each day like nothing's going on (even though there usually is), the whole thing makes me sad and I get depressed. But when I am the saddest and I want desperately to get back the happiness they've taken, I think about something I heard my pastor say in church once: "Sometimes when the world seems the darkest, we need only to look towards the ones we love to find a spark because it's from that spark that your world will once again be lit."

I don't know why I remember this and I don't know that I know exactly what it means, either, but what I do know is it is only because of the people I love that I am able to smile every day, no matter what the bully gang does. They are my spark. Like I said a few days ago, sometimes the weight of the world feels crushing, even for a big guy like me, but with all of that going on I reach for my happy face and get on with the day.

"Stephen," Megan called out to me.

"Hi," I said, smiling, as I walked towards my bus.

"What are you doing?"

"Nothing, why?"

"You want to do nothing with me?"

This suggestion made me a little nervous because hanging with a girl for twenty minutes at lunch was one thing. What was I going to talk to her about for longer than that? Worse yet, what if I can't think of anything to talk about and she finds out that I am a boring jock.

"What do you mean?" I said.

"It's a nice day and since you walk home on nice days I thought we could both walk together."

"I guess," I said, sounding unsure.

"My house is in Farmington Estates. Do you know where that is?"

"Yeah, my bus passes it."

"I know."

"How do you know?" I asked, surprised.

"Toni Sadorni is my writing partner in English class and she told me her house is just down the street from yours."

"That is true."

"I know it's true."

"And your parents won't mind you walking home?"

"I already called them and they said if you are with me then it's okay."

"Really?"

"Really. I told them you look like Superman and they said as long as Superman is with me it's fine."

This made me blush and I felt embarrassed, but what she said she said in a nice way so I didn't mind it too much.

"You didn't really tell them that I look like Superman, did you?" I asked.

"Sure I did, because it's true. The Superman from the original movies, with blond hair, but I think he has blues eyes and yours look brown. Are they brown?"

"Hazel."

She looked at me when she said that and smiled. There was that smile again, with the crooked teeth, but this smile was different somehow, more personal, as if it was just for me. And I suddenly felt like I do when the bases are loaded with no outs. My hands got clammy, my heart beat a little quicker and I felt like I would trip over my words if I tried to speak, like my Aunt Shelia does on New Year's Eve. I looked at her for a second and smiled back.

"You have a nice smile," she said. "It's kind."

"It's kind of what?" I said kiddingly.

"Friendly?"

"Well I'm glad you like it, I like yours too," I said.

Okay, did you ever say something and think to yourself how did that ever come out of my mouth? Well that's what I just did and I really wish I could stuff the words back in.

"Thank you," she said, almost sounding relieved.

"You're welcome," I said, even more relieved that she looked happy that I said it.

Megan was way different than any girl I had ever known. I know my experience with girls is limited, and I know we just met and we haven't spent much time together. I know all of this. But I feel happy when she is around so I'm thinking maybe the baseball field isn't the only place I can be happy. I do know one thing, if Megan had been the girl at the end of the sixty-five mile bike trip Charlie and I started out on, I would not have turned around that day and come home.

"I have to ask you something," I said.

"You sound so serious, what is it?" she asked, looking concerned.

"Where are you from?" I asked.

"That's the question?" Megan started laughing. "I was thinking you were going to ask me something dark and serious."

"You're thirteen, how dark and serious could your life be?"

"I'm actually fourteen."

"Really?" I was surprised that she is older than me. I am one of the oldest kids in my grade and I won't be fourteen for two more months.

"Yep, May third. My birthday just passed, but pink is my favorite color and I like stuffed animals and candy, so remember that for next year."

"I will," I said, smiling.

"Jewelry is nice too. Nothing with diamonds or emeralds though, too fancy. Keep it simple."

"I'll keep that in mind."

"You better," said Megan laughing. "How about you? When's your birthday?"

"I'll be fourteen on the twentieth of July."

"July twentieth?" Megan repeated.

"Yep, July twentieth, and I like basketball sneakers and sunflower seeds."

"Sunflower seeds?" Megan said.

"Yeah, sunflower seeds."

"I won't forget that!"

"You better not."

"I won't, don't worry."

"It's not going to bother you that you're older than me is it?"

"Not at all."

"Good," I said.

"Guys always die before girls anyway," Megan said laughing.

"That's nice." I gave her my best look of fake annoyance.

"Sorry, it's true," she said, and she laughed again.

Megan and I walked and talked and the day was bright and everything felt perfect right up to the moment we stopped at the road leading into her development. I didn't want to act surprised when she told me where she lived earlier, but Farmington Estates is a gated neighborhood with security guards and video cameras at the entrance. The only way into the development is past a guard who stands in a little brick building right in the center of the entrance and exit. The people who own houses in Megan's development are rich -- they drive fancy cars, live in huge houses and obviously like their privacy. Their kids go to private schools like Pemberton Prep or Saint Bernard's Academy, so Megan attending Lamington Public is a big deal. I am sure the kids in school would be just as surprised as me to know that Megan lives here. I don't know how she has kept it a secret, especially since she takes the bus every day. This is the sort of thing that would have been the top line of everyone's gossip list.

"Can I ask you something without you getting angry?" I said.

"I guess it depends on what it is, but let me warn you now, if it's offensive you can't blame me for what I might do."

"What might you do?"

"I don't know, I guess you are going to have to ask your question and we'll see what happens."

"Okay, here it goes. Are you like the maid's kid, or maybe the live-in groundskeeper's daughter?"

Megan's eyes opened really wide and she started to laugh.

"Why is that so funny?" I asked.

"It just is." She couldn't stop laughing.

"So was I right, did I get it? You're the maid's daughter?"

"No, you are not right."

"I thought for sure I was onto something."

"Why?"

"Megan, no one, and I mean *no one*, from Farmington Estates has ever gone to Lamington Public School. No one!"

"I'm a ground breaker," she said proudly.

"Yes you are," I agreed.

"I don't like doing what other people do or what other people expect me to do."

"I've noticed."

"Is that a bad thing?"

"No, but tell me that is not why you friended me," I said, trying not to sound hurt.

It was the first time since I met Megan that I thought my brother Jack might be right. Maybe I am like the injured bird that just flew into the window. Maybe I am her pet project, as my mom would say. Maybe Jack's comment about her taking pity on me wasn't far off.

"That's silly," said Megan.

"Is it?"

"Yes, it is."

"Do you see how I get treated at school?"

"I do and I think it's awful."

"It is awful and you know what, you're putting yourself right in the middle of it."

"No I'm not," Megan said.

"Yes, you are."

"How am I doing that?"

"Once you're seen with me you might get treated the same way."

"I'm not worried about it."

"I am."

At least now that I was thinking about it I am. I was having so much fun with Megan that it didn't dawn on me that her spending time with me could cause her a lot of problems. I suddenly had this impulse to run before it was too late, before someone driving by saw us together.

"I've got to go," I said abruptly.

"Stephen ..."

"I'm sorry, I've got to go. Are you going to be okay from here?"

"Yes, I'll be fine, but are you sure? You can come up to the house with me, I would love for you to come up."

"I'd like to, I really would, but I have a game in a few hours and I have homework to do. Maybe some other time." I didn't really have any homework but I had to get out of there.

"Okay, some other time," she said.

"I'll see you tomorrow," I said.

"Okay, be careful going home."

"Bye Megan."

"Bye," she said, sounding disappointed. "Stephen?"

"Yes?"

"Connecticut."

"Connecticut," I said, not really understanding why she said it.

"You asked me where I was from. I'm from Connecticut."

"Oh." I smiled, then I turned and started to walk away. I fought the urge to turn back around and say, you know what, who cares about Devlin and the bully gang. But I did care and I didn't want her to get hurt.

Chapter 18

The Truth Hurts

I walked the rest of the way home slowly, lost in my thoughts. In the time it took me to get to my house I saw Megan's beautiful crooked smile disappear in my head a million times and I wanted it back. I hurt her feelings, that I knew. I could see it on her face. It had to be the same look I get when the kids are playing pickup basketball and tell me to get lost and won't let me join them. They know I can see that the sides are five against four but they don't want me to play. I can't help but feel like I just did the same exact thing, but I did it to someone I like. It took me a lot longer this time to walk home because I didn't run at all and when I finally made it back, Jack actually looked worried.

"Where have you been?" Jack asked.

"Why?"

"Because you should have been home hours ago."

"I walked again," I said.

"I figured you walked but the last time it didn't take you this long."

"I walked Megan home first."

"I saw you talking to her again but this time you actually walked her home?"

"Yes."

"Did you get to go in her house? Those houses are gigantic aren't they?" Jack said, getting excited.

"No, I didn't go in, and how do you know where she lives?"

"I heard mom talking on the phone."

"When was mom on the phone talking about Megan?"

"Last night."

"And who does mom know that knows Megan?"

"It was one of your teachers."

"Why would one of my teachers be talking to mom about Megan?" I'm sure I was looking at Jack like I thought he was crazy, because that's basically what I was thinking.

"She was actually talking to mom about you."

"What about me?"

"I didn't hear the whole conversation but I think the teacher is concerned about something and wants a conference."

"Yeah, that's not unusual."

"Yeah, but she wanted it right away."

"Why didn't you tell me about this earlier, Bonehead? I thought you said you have my back?" I snapped.

"I do!"

"Really?"

"When was I going to tell you?" Jack demanded.

"This morning."

"At breakfast, with Dad sitting right there?"

"Okay, so after."

"We were on the bus after, should I have told you in front of everyone?"

"No, I guess not. Where is Mom now?"

"She's at the school. I told you they wanted to talk to her right away."

"She came home from work?" I asked. Now I was starting to worry.

"Yes, and then she went to the school."

"Did she ask where I was?"

"Yes."

"What did you tell her?"

"I said the last time I saw you was at school with Megan and that you didn't get on the bus. I had to tell her, what else was I going to say?"

"Jack, it's no big deal, chill."

"Stephen, there is something else," Jack said. He sounded pretty serious.

"What is it?"

"Did you know that Megan moved here from Connecticut?"

"Yeah, why?"

"Did she tell you why she moved here?"

"No, but it looks like you're going to tell me and the way you're going about it sounds like it's not good."

"Megan is from Greens Farms, Connecticut, which is an affluent area very similar to here."

"Affluent? Come on, Jack, English please."

"Sorry, rich. She's from an area with money," Jack explained.

I shrugged. "So what, her parents have money. Where would you expect them to live?"

"I know that, I was just giving you some detail."

"Well get to the point, Jack."

"I have to show you something because if I just tell you're not going to believe me anyway."

"So show me."

I followed Jack to his bedroom where he sat down at his computer and Googled "Connecticut Milton." When all the information popped up on the page, Jack scrolled down until he came to what he was looking for. The news headline read "Philanthropist Douglas A. Milton's Daughter…". Jack clicked on the headline and we waited until the news story came up on the screen, along with two pictures. One photo was of Megan's dad, who looked similarly dressed to Jeffrey on a Friday, and the other was of Megan. Megan's photo looked like it might have been copied out of her school yearbook. She was all decked out in a school uniform so now I know that at one time she did attend one of those prep schools.

The internet news headline read in full, "Philanthropist Douglas A. Milton's Daughter Attempts Suicide." Megan's name wasn't mentioned in the headline so, even though it took me by surprise, it also could have been a sister. As I read the story, I learned that a group of five teens had been charged last year after "the daughter" of Douglas A. Milton attempted suicide. From statements made by friends and family of "Miss Milton", the police determined that the boys had been bullying "Miss Milton" for some time. The boys were being held in a juvenile detention center awaiting criminal charges for posting and possessing inappropriate photos of "the teenage girl." The photos were taken without the consent or knowledge of "the teen" and then posted on several internet sites. According to this article the charges against the boys were very serious.

"Stephen, are you all right?" Jack asked after I had been quiet for a while.

"Jack, it never says Megan's name. Maybe it wasn't Megan."

"Stephen."

"What? The article also says the girl was a seventh grader and Megan is in seventh grade now."

"It was Megan, Stephen. It's her picture in the article."

"Maybe that's not her in the photo. How do you know?" I said, starting to get choked up.

"Mom. I heard Mom talking to Dad."

My mom doesn't usually get a story straight so normally I would have rolled my eyes and taken comfort with that thought, but not today. Today I stood in my brother's tiny room with my hand over my mouth, shocked. I was fighting back the emotion and the pain that was flooding over me. I even read the story again, hoping it wasn't true, but with every word I read I felt sicker and more nauseous. And then the one thing I hate the most in the whole world happened. Maybe it had to do with how badly I felt for Megan or maybe it had to do with me as well, but I started to cry. I held it in the best I could but it wouldn't stay there. I ran out of my brother's room and into my own, shutting and locking the door. I threw myself onto my bed, burying my face in my pillow, and I cried. I cried for Megan, I cried for Jack, I cried for me, and I cried for everyone who has ever had to live like this.

Chapter 19

Stephen VS. Dodgers

I went into that night's game against the Dodgers totally consumed with anger. Every face I saw on their team made me more and more mad because I wasn't seeing the real players. I saw the five boys from Connecticut, even though I had no idea what they looked like. I saw each and every kid in my school who takes part in bullying, and not just the ones who bully me, all of them.

In the first inning I singled to left field, knocking in two runs, and then, like a bull set loose in the street, I stole second and then third and then, on a short hop to the shortstop, I ran home. This wasn't a ball that I would have normally run on but I did anyway and, as the catcher braced himself to make the play at home, I ran like a train right at him. And this train would not stop; not for Devlin, not for Kevin and certainly not for someone getting in the way of home plate. I was like a pickup truck with no brakes heading right for the kid on a bicycle and I plowed him over, knocking the ball down the first base line. With my size, running over the catcher was like running over a squirrel in your car -- you know your mom just did it, you can see her cringing in the driver's seat, but you didn't feel a thing. I was called safe at home and the Dodger's coach screamed foul on me but it was ruled a legal play and the run counted.

In the third inning I made it easy on everyone and just knocked the ball into the parking lot, leaving no casualties behind. But in the fifth inning, with nobody on base, the Dodgers decided they would rather walk me than pitch to me. I didn't care. I stole second base on the first pitch to the next batter, third base on the second pitch, and now I was staring down their brand new catcher. I took a short lead off of third and when the next pitch went into the dirt past the catcher, I chugged away towards home. I could see the pitcher start to make his move to cover home but when the catcher turned to make his throw there was no one to throw to. The pitcher was lucky if he weighed a hundred and sixty pounds dripping wet, so I guess after seeing what I did to the first catcher, he didn't even bother to try and make the play. The fact that he just let me score did not sit well with his coach because the coach screamed at him at the top of his lungs and ended up taking him out of the game.

In the seventh inning I stood at home plate for a long time when it was my turn to bat, thinking of Megan and thinking of those boys. I stepped out of the box twice before I cleared my head enough to swing, and with all the anger pent up in me, I hit the next pitch farther than I have ever hit a ball before. I ran and watched the ball sail through the air as I stepped on first base with unnecessary force, hoping to squash all the hate away. I hit second base seeing Megan's face, and third sharing in her pain, and when I got to home I leaped in the air and landed on home plate with both feet ... and felt nothing. I looked around and saw everyone celebrating what should have been my moment. They were screaming and clapping and I realized sadly that I hadn't had any fun. It didn't matter that I had hit two home runs. I didn't feel happy that we won (Giants 15, Dodgers 4). It was the first baseball game that I could ever remember playing, win or lose, where it just wasn't fun.

Chapter 20

The Heart of the Matter

The ride home with my dad was a quiet one and I wasn't sure why. I don't know if he sensed there was something wrong or if he knew by the way I played but he just let it hang there without saying anything. He made a left out of the parking lot, going the opposite way of home, and the car followed the road's twists and turns for a few miles before he began to slow down. Lamington Lake was coming up and the entrance to the state park was right in front of us. Without saying a word or giving me a reason, Dad turned onto Lake Road and followed it until the road ended at the boat launch area. He threw his car into reverse and we moved backwards until he was in a spot facing the lake. He turned off the engine and got out of the car. The first time he spoke was as he opened my car door and it was only to ask me to join him. He slid himself up onto the hood of his car and I followed him, both of us looking out at the lake and watching as the sun began to set behind the mountains. We watched the sky change colors for a few minutes before he spoke again.

"I can't help you if you don't talk to me, Stephen."

"I do talk to you, Dad."

"No, I mean really talk to me," he said.

"I do really talk to you."

"No, you don't. We talk about baseball or movies that you've seen. We go over school things and what you should or shouldn't be doing, whether you are studying, are you reading."

"Those are all important."

"True, but there are other things that you can share with me and your mom."

"Like what?"

"Like what is really going on in your life right now, that's what."

"There is nothing going on."

"Okay, let's say that's true. Then tell me what was going on with you *tonight*."

"What do you mean?"

My dad let out a deep breath before continuing,

"Stephen, I have been watching you play ball since you were a little boy. I've seen you play on your worst days and I have seen you play on your best. But tonight I watched a stranger playing and that concerns me."

"I played well," I said in my own defense.

"I didn't say that you played poorly, I said that I didn't know that boy. You were not the Stephen I know."

"Who was I?"

"You tell me, that's what I'm asking."

"I'm just me. Stephen."

"My Stephen would never have leveled that catcher, never."

"He had the plate blocked."

"I didn't say it was a dirty hit, but you put that boy in the emergency room. I don't know if you know that, but that is where he is right now, legal hit or not."

"I didn't know that," I said softly. I felt bad.

"I didn't think you did."

"I didn't mean for that to happen."

"I know you didn't, but that *is* what happened and I want to know why."

"I was mad."

"At who?"

"Some boys."

"What boys?"

"The boys that hurt Megan," I said, and then it happened again. I tried to stop myself but my feelings just wouldn't stay locked up. So I cried. I know it's embarrassing, but I did it anyway.

My dad put his hand on my shoulder and listened as I told him about the news article Jack had shown me on the internet. He said he had already seen it and he felt bad for Megan too. I asked him about my mom meeting with the teacher to talk about me but he wouldn't tell me who the teacher was or if Megan was mentioned. I talked about Megan a little and what she was like but I didn't tell him about leaving Megan standing at the entrance to her development. If I told him that then I would have to explain why and then I would have to tell him about the bullying going on at school.

That's right, my parents don't know because that's how I want it. I know what you're thinking: if I were him, I would just tell on those kids and then everything would be good in Stephen's world. But what if I tell and it makes it worse? And don't tell me it can't be worse, look what those boys did to Megan.

My dad said that he thinks my friendship with Megan is a good thing, and that after what Megan's been through I should feel special that she reached out to me to be a friend. He also thinks this had to be hard for her to do since trusting people would be difficult after what happened to her. Wow, now I felt really bad about how I left things with Megan.

Talking to my dad at the lake helped me sort out my day and I went to bed feeling a little better, but I still felt conflicted too. I want to stay friends with Megan but I don't want her to end up being bullied again because of me. I'm just not really sure what I should do.

Chapter 21

Doing Something

I hadn't seen Megan all day long and I even went out of my way to look. At lunch I sat in the cafeteria eating double helpings of some meat concoction the school cooks had put together, hoping that she would show up, but she never did. I went into the library and walked around, checking out every aisle, but no Megan. It wasn't until the last period of the day, when I was in the middle of plowing over poor James Ferrel, the catcher from last night's game, for the hundredth time that she finally showed up and the sound of her voice instantly snapped me back to class. She walked up to Miss Stanton and handed her a note of some kind, then she turned and looked right at me. My heart sank when she gave me this huge smile and waved. She seemed happy to see me. Didn't she remember yesterday? I was the boy who dumped her at the curb and took off. I know it wasn't that drastic but it felt like it to me, and I thought she might have felt that way too.

"Hi," she whispered from behind me, after she was sitting at her desk.

I waved to her over my shoulder without turning around. When

class was over I turned and she was writing some numbers down on a piece of paper.

"Hi," I said, smiling.

"Hello."

"What are you doing after school?"

"Nothing," she said, "why do you ask?"

"I thought you might want to do nothing with me," I said, hoping to amuse her.

"I don't know, we did nothing yesterday and it didn't go so well."

"Okay, that hurt," I said laughing. I was laughing on the outside but very nervous on the inside, especially since she just seemed to confirm that leaving her on the curb didn't make a good impression.

"I'm kidding," she said jokingly.

"Well then how about we do something?" I said.

"Like what?"

"I don't know, I was scheduled to do nothing but I can work something into my schedule. We can walk and talk about it."

"Sounds fun, but I have to talk to Miss Stanton before I leave."

"Okay, I will meet you outside," I said while loading my backpack.

"I figured that," Megan said, smiling.

As I waited outside for Megan my brother came running out of the school heading for the bus. He was loaded down with his backpack and trombone case and he tried to wave at me, but when that didn't work, he walked over to talk to me instead.

"You coming?" Jack asked

"No, I'm walking home."

"Alone?"

"What do you think?" I said, smiling.

"Nice," he said. "Go in the house this time."

"We'll see."

"What should I tell mom?"

"I'll be home before her."

"What if you're not? Then what should I say?"

"Tell mom I will call her if I'll be late but not to worry, they have guards at the gate."

"Really?" Jack said, surprised.

"Yes, really. Now go! You're going to miss the bus."

"I could walk with you," Jack suggested.

"I don't think so."

"I was just kidding." Jack said. "Get a sense of humor."

"Sorry, I'll see you later."

"Bye."

The buses were all long gone when Megan finally came out so we walked a little faster today. I had already promised myself that I would not leave her at the gate this time, no matter what.

"You want to come up or do you have baseball tonight?" Megan asked as we got to her street.

"I can come up for a little while. Do I need ID to get in?" I said smiling.

"Not if you know the right people," she teased.

"Are you the right people?"

"Follow me," she said and then took my hand, pulling me towards the guard house.

The guard must have seen us coming because he had already begun to step out of his little house to greet us. I do have to say, the word "guard" here is used very loosely. When I hear the word I picture a big bad dude with lots of muscles, not some grandfatherly-type guy with a flashlight in his belt where a gun should be.

"Good afternoon, Miss Milton," the guard said politely.

"Hi, Gus."

"Who do you have with you?" Gus asked.

"Gus, this is Stephen."

"Stephen," the guard said, pausing. "Why do you look familiar?"

"I don't know," I said, shrugging my shoulders.

"It's because he looks like Superman," Megan said.

"She's right, you do look like Superman! I'll be darned, we have a young Christopher Reeves on the property. Well, I guess if you have Superman with you today, you won't need me to protect you."

"I always need you, Gus," Megan said in a sort of flirty manner.

Megan is amazing with people. Unlike me, she always seems at ease and knows all the right things to say. As I watched her talk to Gus, I realized how delicate she looks. Like a porcelain angel or something, and yet powerful at the same time. Not powerful like Charlie's mom, in that pit bull way, but just sure of herself in a way that makes her seem strong. It's hard for me to imagine that she could ever have wanted to hurt herself. She looks like she is on top of the world and no one could knock her down. Or maybe she's like me and when she wakes up every day she slips on that happy face. A happy Halloween mask with a smile that is just too big and perfect to be real.

"You coming?" I heard Megan say. She had walked ahead of me a few steps.

"Following you," I replied.

"Nice meeting you, Stephen. If you run into any trouble fighting the bad guys, give me a call. I still have a little fight in me yet," Gus said.

I laughed and said, "I will do that."

As we walked away from the guard house, I said to Megan, "He's a funny guy."

"He is really nice. His wife died in March so I think the last few months have been really hard for him."

"You would never know, he seems perfectly fine."

"I know," Megan said sadly.

Chapter 22

A Taste of Bad

After school the basketball court was being taken up by Devlin and the bully gang with no sign of Jeffrey.

"What happened to the dweeb?" Devlin said.

"Which one is that?" Kevin said laughing.

"Jeffrey," Devlin said, "I thought for sure he would come. He looked like he was going to fall over when I asked him to play again today."

"He told me he has a surprise for us, one he thinks we'll like."

"Hopefully it not just a bag of Twizzlers like that dork Stephen brings to school all the time."

"Hey, don't trash the Twizzlers. I like Twizzlers," said Kevin.

"I do too, but he could bring something different occasionally. What does his mom do anyway, work at the Twizzler factory?"

"I don't know and I don't care. He shares them with everyone, doesn't he?"

"Yep."

"So what do we care where he gets them from?"

"I guess we don't," said Devlin, as he took a three point shot that

landed dead center of the hoop and swished through the net.

“How do you do that all the time?” Kevin said, shaking his head in amazement.

“Skill dude, it’s all skill.”

“Well share some of that with me.”

“Sorry, I don’t share, you will have to get your own,” Devlin said laughing.

Chapter 23

The Whole Truth

Megan's home looked more like a resort than a house. It was large enough to squeeze half the houses on my street into. Her driveway was paved with little odd-shaped cobblestones and as it made its way up to the house it split in two opposite directions which eventually joined back up, making a circle with a patch of grass in the center the size of a small park. A few trees and bushes were planted, giving some life to the grassy area, and there were two fountains, each one not quite in the middle, like candle holders decorating the dining room table. These fountains were spraying water into the air as we walked by.

The front of the house was a mix of stone and stucco. It was all done so that the stone popped out a little. It looked amazing. It kind of reminded me of photos I had seen in my history text book of buildings in Italy. The house had big white columns and a few archways and it had more windows than my whole school. It really looked like it was built for a king or the President, or a movie star.

"Wow! You actually live here?" I said.

"We just moved in last month but my mom and dad have been

getting it ready since February."

"What did they have to do to it? It looks perfect."

"They had it painted and the floors were refinished, and my mom had to shop for furniture and stuff. All that took time."

"It's awesome!"

"It's just a house."

"A *really nice* house."

"You have a nice house too," Megan said, sounding a little uncomfortable.

"It's nothing like this!"

"Yes, I know, but it's still nice. I've seen it," Megan said.

"You've seen my house?" I said, feeling a little embarrassed.

"I have."

"When?"

"A few weeks ago. I told you that Toni is my writing partner. We have been working on a project together and one day when I was at her house she and I walked around town. She pointed out where people live who I might know from school and there was your house."

"It's small."

"It's perfect."

"No, *this* is perfect."

"It's too much. How many rooms in your house do you spend time in?"

"I don't know, probably three or four."

"Let me guess which ones."

"Okay."

"Most kids spend time in their bedrooms so that is one," Megan began.

"That's correct."

"Now everyone's house is different but everyone has some sort of a family area where they watch TV so that is my second guess."

"You've got two," I said.

"Judging from your size you know where they keep the food so my third guess is the kitchen, and the fourth is wherever your family eats dinner. Am I right?" Megan said, smiling.

"Well, in my house we actually eat dinner in the kitchen, but yes, you got it." I smiled back at her.

"And what rooms of my house do you think I spend my time in?"

"Probably the same as me?"

"That is correct. So it is my opinion that if you took away all the extra rooms in my house, your house and mine are much more similar than you think."

"You have a bizarre way of thinking," I said.

"It's not bizarre, it's realistic."

"I like the fountains, they're cool," I said, turning to look at them.

"That's funny, because they are one of my favorite parts of this house too. Come with me, I want to show you something."

Megan took my hand and pulled me toward the fountains. Alongside each fountain is a cement bench with big rocks set next to each end.

"Sit down, I'll be right back," she said. "This is much prettier at night but I still think you will like it."

Megan took off running and from where I was sitting it looked like she was going to jump into a hedgerow of bushes. Instead she stopped, and fumbled around with something behind the bushes.

"Are you ready?" she called out.

"Yeah, I guess," I answered.

Then suddenly, the fountain water started to turn different colors and the water started squirting at different times and at different angles. It was pretty amazing to watch, and then music started playing. I have no idea where the music was coming from, but it sounded cool. Megan came back and sat down next to me.

"It really is much prettier at night," she said.

"No, it's cool," I said.

"Wait until you see the water do circles."

"I wish I had one of these at my house," I said.

"I'll buy you one for your birthday. I know when it is," she said and winked at me.

The music Megan turned on was like something you would hear in a movie, when there's some big dramatic moment happening. There were no vocals, just piano and violins.

"This music is perfect with the way the water is moving," I said. It was very pretty to listen to.

"I know, I really like it too," Megan said cheerfully.

"Is this music from a movie?" I asked.

"You don't recognize it?"

"Why would I recognize it?" I asked, surprised by her

question.

"I was told that you like this music," Megan explained.

"Are you messing with me?"

"No, I heard that you like Liberace. That's why I picked this song."

"This is Liberace?"

"Yes."

"Did Charlie tell you about Liberace?"

"No, I've never met Charlie."

"He didn't introduce himself and then get you to put on Liberace?"

"Stephen, I don't understand, why would he do that?"

"To be funny." Of course, I didn't find it at all funny.

"To be honest, I heard little Jeffrey talking about it and I thought that I would surprise you," Megan said.

"Jeffrey Talin?" I said, sounding shocked.

"Yes, it was Jeffrey."

"Can you turn it off please?"

"Sure, but why?"

Before I could answer, Megan got up and turned the music off. When she got back, I said,

"I asked you the other day if you saw the way I was being treated at school."

"And I said yes. I think it's terrible."

"But this is part of it."

"Stephen, I don't understand what this has to do with that."

"Megan, they send me stuff in the mail."

"Who, Miss Stanton?" Megan said looking puzzled.

"No, the kids do! Why would Miss Stanton send me things in the mail?"

"The kids do?" said Megan as the realization set in.

"Some kids in class send me things in the mail. Nasty notes, magazines, and the music you just put on, Liberace, was a gift from them. I don't listen to Liberace, I didn't know who Liberace was until they sent the CDs. Yesterday I got seed packets in the mail to grow pansies and pussy willows. Do you think they are trying to tell me something?"

"Oh Stephen, I am so sorry! I thought you were talking about the way Miss Stanton was treating you. I didn't know."

"Megan, no one knows about the CDs but me and Charlie, and I know he would never tell anyone, so the only way Jeffrey could know is if he was in on it."

"They're bullying you?" Megan sounded shocked.

"Yes."

"Who?"

"I only know who some of them are but I'm sure there are others. They do everything anonymously so anyone could be in on it. I never would have suspected Jeffrey though."

"How long have they been doing this?"

"It's been going on to some degree for years, but it has gotten much worse over the last year."

"Do you know why?"

"No, I can't think of anything I ever did that would have started this."

"I told a boy no," Megan said very matter of factly.

"What?" I had no idea what she was talking about.

"That's why we moved from Connecticut," she continued.

"Why?"

"My best friend's brother asked me out and I told him no. I had just turned twelve and I didn't want to go out with anyone, and even if I did, my parents weren't going to let me start dating at twelve. So I told him no and he hated me for it. For a year after that, he and his friends picked on me in school."

"So you moved to get away from them?"

"Yes and no."

"What do you mean?"

Megan looked down at the ground and you could tell that whatever she was thinking was sort of stuck on her tongue and reluctant to come out. Finally, still staring at the ground, she said,

"One of my friends had a swim party and my friends were all like me, kids from money. Stephanie had a beautiful pool and in the bottom part of her house there was a fitness room with ladies' and men's locker rooms. At the party we went into the locker room a bunch of times, changing in and out of our bathing suits and to shower when we were all done."

Megan stopped talking and her hand shot up to her mouth and tears started to fall down her cheeks. I didn't really know what to do. I had never had to watch a girl cry before. And to make matters worse, I know the story she was telling. I know how it ends. I read it on the internet and I could have told her right off so she didn't have to relive it. But it was personal and none of my business. And

I also didn't want her to know that I knew. Why do things have to be so complicated?

She was still crying, but she continued her story,

"I didn't know Stephanie's brother was friends with those other boys, but he was. A week after the party they posted videos and photos of me while I was in that dressing room all over the internet. I came into school one day and the kids were all laughing at me and I didn't know why. But during the day I started to get calls on my cell from men saying they saw my ad and my photos on the web and they wanted to set up a time to meet. I asked one of the men what site he was talking about and then I Googled it and there I was, Megan Milton for sale. They even posted my real name.

As it turns out, my friend Stephanie had helped her brother and his friends wire the locker room with spy cameras. I have no idea why she would do that, but she did, so they got pictures of almost all the girls at the party. But mine they took and posted on every site they could get them on. After I found the website on my phone I ran out of school and I never wanted to see anyone there again."

She stopped talking again, and I felt like I should say something.

"Megan, you don't have to tell me any more," I said.

She looked up at me and kept talking. "I got home and went up to my room."

"Megan, you don't …"

"I was so embarrassed and it hurt so badly. I couldn't' stand the pain. What they did I could never get away from."

"Megan …"

"I could never go back to school. I could never look my friends in the eyes again and I couldn't get the laughing out of my head."

"I am so sorry." I didn't know what else to say.

"They ruined my life, or that's what I was thinking, so I thought the only way out was … ." She paused and shook her head.

"To die," I said softly.

"Yes."

"I know how that feels."

"I'm sorry."

"Me too."

"And that's why we moved."

"It's a new start," I said.

"With new friends," Megan said, now starting to smile.

"With new friends," I said, smiling with her.

The scary part of all of this is that the Megan I know is confident, happy and full of life and, after spending more time with her, I am sure she is not just slipping on that smiley mask every day like I am. My situation caught her by surprise and at the same time it brought up some bad memories and some tears, but the strong Megan has returned to stay. That crooked smile I like so much is real and comes from her heart, beaming like sunshine. So now I'm sure you're asking, what's the scary part in that? Okay, here it is: what if Megan's plan to die had worked? I would have never met the happy Megan that I know and that, to me, is scary.

Chapter 24

Gum With a Kick

Since I hadn't heard from Charlie in two days I finally decided to give him a call and see what he was up to.

"Can you come out?"

"Sure, want me to bring my glove?" he asked.

"Why not."

* * *

"So where have you been?"

"Putting around," Charlie said with a smile.

"Putting around where? I haven't seen you at school in two days?"

"That's because I haven't been there in two days."

"With finals coming up your mom let you take off for two days? I find that hard to believe," I said.

"Okay, I am going to tell you something that you have to promise you will keep to yourself," Charlie said while glancing up and down our street.

"How long have you known me?"

"Still, I'm going to need a pinky swear for this."

"Aren't we a little old for pinky swears?"

"We are, but I'm bringing it back for just this one time."

"It must be a big secret!"

"It's huge."

"Okay you got me, I pinky swear."

And me and Charlie both reached up and hooked our pinkies together, something that we haven't done since we were little kids.

"Okay, now tell me, what's with all the mystery?" I asked.

"Well, remember the other night when my mom came out screaming at me?"

"Yeah, I believe she told you not to vart," I said laughing.

"If you make fun I'm not going to tell you."

"I'm not making fun, that is what she said."

"No, she said don't fart."

"It was vart, but move on."

"Well the reason she was screaming at me is the gum I had been chewing was supposed to go to my grandmother."

"You took your grandmother's gum? That's terrible! How could you do that to your grandmother?" I said, laughing again.

"It gets worse."

"How?"

"Well, my grandmother has been constipated because of some medicine she's taking."

"Constipated?" I said.

"Yes, constipated. It's when your poop gets stuck."

"It gets stuck where?"

"Inside you. You feel like you have to go but you can't squeeze one out."

"I know what it is, I'm just messing with you. Geez, Charlie! What does that have to do with the gum and you farting?"

"Well, it was a special kind of gum."

"Are you trying to say it's a type of gum that makes you poop?"

"Yes, that is what I am trying to say."

"I have never heard of such a thing," I said with disbelief.

"Well they make it and I was chewing it while we were playing catch the other night," Charlie insisted.

"Did it make you poop?"

"When I was going into the house I had this real bad urge."

"What kind of urge?"

"I needed to fart."

"But your mom told you not to fart." I laughed again, I couldn't help it.

"I know, but do you do everything your mom tells you to do?"

"Of course not."

"Well neither do I."

"So you farted."

"Man, I let one rip that you could hear echo throughout the house."

"So what happened?" I asked. I knew there had to be more.

"Do you know when a fart is not a fart?"

"No, when?"

"When it is diarrhea."

"I don't get it."

"I pooped my pants."

"When you farted?"

"Yes. It was dripping down my legs and stuck to my pants."

"Okay, I get it."

"It was so nasty," Charlie said, making a grossed out face.

"Well *that* will teach you not to steal from your grandmother."

"Yes it will."

"What's the gum called?"

"Laxi-Gum."

"And the name didn't give you a clue?"

"My mom's from Holland, she shops at the Dutch store in Flemington sometimes so I don't understand all the labels. They're written in Dutch. I just saw the word gum."

"So did your poor grandmother get her gum?"

"No."

"Why not?"

"I chewed it all."

"You're kidding?" I said, shocked. "You told your mother you only had a few pieces, I heard you."

"I lied. I had stuffed the whole pack in my mouth."

"No way."

"Yes way."

"Did she have to take you to the hospital?" I asked.

"No, I couldn't go to the hospital."

"Why not?"

"I couldn't stop pooping, that's why not. I was stuck in the bathroom."

"So what did your mom do?"

"She called the doctor and they told her just to watch for excessive bloating, and if there was any bleeding to bring me in."

"So you have been pooping for two days?"

"Two days!" Charlie said, sounding almost proud.

"So what have you been doing besides pooping?"

"Listening to music."

"Anything good?"

"I was jamming out to my new Liberace CDs."

I gave Charlie a look. "You know that's not funny."

"I know, sorry. Have they sent you anything new?" he asked.

As a matter of fact, I had gotten a package in the mail from the Virginia Seed Company, so I told Charlie about it and the two different types of seeds that were in it. Of course these seeds were not sent to me for planting purposes, though both pansies and pussy willows are very nice plants. Again the bully gang was sending their message and I was receiving it loud and clear. But as I stood there telling Charlie about the seeds, something crossed my mind. Plants grow best when they're planted in rich soil and the best soil usually contains fertilizer. I don't know if you have ever smelled the air after a farmer's field has been fertilized but it smells really bad and that's because some farms use manure, which is basically animal crap, as fertilizer. I know the word crap doesn't sound good, and my mom yells at me if she hears me say it, but I think I have taken a lot more crap from these kids than anyone should ever have to.

"Charlie," I said, "what was the name of that gum again?"

I mean really, isn't crap just a little poop?

I know what you're thinking to yourself right now, Stephen, don't do it. Be the bigger man boy and walk away. But in my mind it was too late to just walk away and keep doing nothing. At that moment I wasn't really thinking straight and I saw the opportunity to get even with these kids. I know it would never come close to evening the score between them and me, but I honestly thought it would be a harmless way to get a little payback. Charlie had just chewed a whole package of Laxi-Gum and he's okay. So if the normal dose is two pieces and they stay within the safety limits on the warning label everything should be fine. Except for the pooping.

Chapter 25

The Cycle

Giants VS. Pirates

I am sure that I had a huge smile on my face as I stepped on home plate for the fourth time of the game. And I have to say that my mom is right, smiling really does make you feel happy. I had only hit for the cycle one other time in my whole little league career and it was a tremendous feeling to round the bases knowing that I had just done it again. Now I don't want to make it sound like I have never had four hits in a game before because I have already done that this season. I have even had five hits in a game, but there is just something cool about hitting for the cycle. I don't know if you know what that is, but when you hit for the cycle it means that you've gotten every type of hit that can be recorded in a baseball game (a single, double, triple and home run), and it doesn't have to be done in any particular order either. We went on to beat the Pirates 15-4 and I can only say I wish that happy feeling could just stay with me and never leave. It was like wearing flannel pajamas on a cold day. But unfortunately, even flannel pajamas have to come off.

Chapter 26

Crunch Time

There isn't' much time left in the school year and it is crunch time. We are all preparing for final exams and finishing up projects. One of those for me is an essay on Lewis and Clark which is due tomorrow. The text books we started out the year with are now running out of pages, and all the information we've covered is supposed to be neatly folded and stacked like tiny little shirts on a shelf in our brains. But in my brain the clothes are mostly still in one giant heap on the floor.

The essay I was finishing up is for Miss Stanton's class. It was hard but I'm feeling pretty good about it. It has to be five pages long and it has to be typed, with double spaces and required indentions and margins. Miss Stanton is a stickler for detail and any little mistake in format will mean points taken away.

The hardest part of writing for me, other than all of it, is finding a way to put ideas in my own words and not copy directly from the text book. I found that I had done that a couple of times so I reworked those parts, and as I was finishing typing the essay on the computer I tried to read it carefully to make sure I didn't miss anything.

By 11pm I was tired but I was done. I had all five pages printed out and arranged in order, ready to be hole-punched and put into my newly purchased essay binder. We had to stop at the store to buy it on the way to tonight's game (with my mom questioning why I had waited until the last minute to tell her I needed it). While I was at the store I also bought six packs of gum and some sunflower seeds, which I ran out of in the fifth inning of the game. When my head hits the pillow at night my last thought is usually about baseball, but tonight I just saw gum.

Chapter 27

Prepared for the Switch

Jeffrey walked into school with the confidence of a varsity quarterback, standing tall (or at least as tall as he could make five feet look) and moving with a purpose. He was feeling proud of his plan. He was even wearing his Friday tie on Thursday for effect.

Jeffrey had also gone to the store the night before and his purchase consisted of every color essay binder that they had. In each binder he put an essay on Lewis and Clark by Stephen Miller. It was the same essay in each binder, which Jeffrey made sure was not so perfectly typed or spaced and didn't follow many of Miss Stanton's rules. Not only would Stephen get an F on this essay, but in Jeffrey's version, he had copied and plagiarized excerpts of the text throughout. The only variable now was how Jeffrey could switch folders without being seen.

"Jeffrey," Kevin called out.

"Hi," Jeffrey said with a grin.

"What's with you?"

"What do mean by that?" said Jeffrey.

"You've got on your Friday tie."

"I always wear this tie on special occasions."

"It's Thursday, what's so special about today?"

"The surprise," Jeffrey said, patting his backpack.

"Oh, the surprise," Kevin said knowingly.

"I need your help though," Jeffrey said.

Kevin thought, help? That was not in the game plan. He is supposed to stay neutral; no involvement is what Devlin said. Now the dweeb wants help.

"What kind of help?" asked Kevin.

"I don't know how Miss Stanton intends to collect the essays. If we all pass them forward I can make the switch when he hands his to me, but if we just drop them on her desk on the way out of class I'm going to need a second to switch the binders. If that's what happens, I will try to get directly behind Stephen. Then, if the rest of you just pile up behind me, I can do it safely."

"That's it?"

"That's all I need."

"What if she just walks around and collects them?"

"Yeah, that's the third possibility but I don't have that one worked out yet."

"Dude, are you kidding?"

"I'm working on it."

"That's a big hole."

"Don't worry, I will figure it out."

"I'm not worried, it's your thing. I just would hate to see you get this far and mess it up, that's all."

"I am not going to mess anything up," Jeffrey said, annoyed by Kevin's comment.

"Okay then."

Chapter 28

The Voice of Reason

For years Charlie has stood by my side as I've been bullied by these kids and he's hated it. He has often said that he doesn't understand why I haven't walked up to Devlin, their leader, and knocked his teeth out. He said that once you take out the commander the rest would duck and run. Yes, Charlie was definitely in my corner, so if I could trust and confide in anyone, it was him. I also knew that he would tell me exactly what he thought about things, no holds barred. That's why I decided to tell him about my plan.

"That is the stupidest idea I have ever heard," Charlie said.

"Why is it stupid?" I demanded.

"For one, you might get suspended."

"So what? We only have two weeks left," I reasoned.

"How about baseball? Those kids' parents are going to scream so loud that they are going to have to find a way to punish you."

"But school and baseball have no connection," I said.

"Sure they do. They are both run by the town and if they want to they could suspend you from the team."

"You sure?"

"Don't you remember when Phil Jazic stuck the dead rat in the teacher's lounge?"

"I do."

"He was our second basemen at the time and after the rat he was gone for the whole season."

"I didn't realize that."

"Well, he was, so don't do it. They aren't worth it. You have walked away from them so many times, why start fighting back now?"

"I don't know," I admitted.

"Stephen, have I ever steered you wrong before?

"Yes."

"Ha! That's true, I don't even know why I said that."

"Because you're an idiot."

"Do you really want to compare report cards?"

"No not really."

"Anyway, just take their seeds and walk away. Plant some pansies and pussy willows, plop your lounge chair in the middle of them and listen to some Liberace music. They paid for it all so you might as well enjoy it. You did say the music sounded good with the water show at Megan's," Charlie said laughing.

"I think you should remember that I can kick your butt," I said.

"That is true, but then you wouldn't have me to talk you out of doing stupid things."

"Yes, that's true."

"So it's agreed, you're not going to do this, right?" Charlie asked.

"No, I guess you're right," I said.

"Good, now give me the gum," Charlie said, reaching out his hand.

"Why?"

"Stephen, I can see you changing your mind."

"I won't."

"You're right, you won't, especially if you don't have it on you. Then it won't matter if the thought pops up in your head again. Now give it up."

"Okay, but you're not going to chew it are you?"

"Are you kidding? My butt is still sore from the last time."

Charlie was right, it was a bad idea. He was also right that if I didn't have the gum with me I wouldn't be tempted to carry out my plan, so I handed it over.

"Stephen, you have three packs of real gum too?" Charlie asked. He saw me take them out when I was getting the pooping gum.

"I do. I was going to put the Laxi-Gum into the peppermint gum packs since they are exactly the same size."

"Well, you don't need three packs of gum do you?"

"No, I don't even like peppermint."

"I do. Can I have at least one pack?"

"Take them all," I said as I handed them over.

"Thanks, and you will thank me for this one day."

"Maybe," I said.

As I stood up to leave the cafeteria, I suddenly lost the high I was feeling when I got up this morning. I had come to school all revved up for payback and now it's back to idle. I'm back to just stepping out of their way again.

I looked over my shoulder on my way out and I could see Devlin and the bully gang sitting there and laughing. Jeffrey was sitting with them, having a good old time, and I think maybe somewhere inside I wished that were me. Okay, not really. I also saw Charlie, who had moved and was now wearing his Ray-Ban sunglasses, sitting and talking with Peggy Sloan. He was smiling. I thought Peggy was history. I would have to ask him about that later.

Chapter 29

The Switch

My dad just bought a new car, and I don't know if you have ever noticed this when your family has gotten one, but suddenly I see that model car all over the place. I never even knew the car existed before the day my dad drove it home but now it is everywhere I look. I guess I'm telling you this because I think it's the same with people. Since I met Megan she seems to pop up a lot more often.

"Megan," I hollered as I was walking up the hallway.

"Stephen," Megan said, smiling as she shut her locker. "You scared me."

"Sorry, I just thought we could walk to class together."

"Sure we can."

"You know what's funny? I have walked down this hallway so many times and this is the first time I've ever seen you at your locker."

"You need to pay better attention because I have seen you at yours a million times."

"You have?"

"Yes. Should I feel hurt that you haven't noticed me?" she

said.

"No," I said, feeling a little guilty.

"I am only kidding. Toni's locker is right next to yours so I see you every time I go to meet her before English class."

"That's right, I forgot you two are friends. You are friends, right?"

"Yes, we are, now let's go before we're late."

Megan pulled on my arm to get me moving and just as we started walking to class we heard voices coming down the hall. It was Devlin and the bully gang.

"Let's go the other way," I said to Megan.

"Stephen, no. This way is faster, and you can't keep worrying about me," Megan said, insisting.

Jeffrey was the first one to turn the corner. I don't know what it was but he looked nervous when he saw me standing there. And if he knew that I knew about him being one of them, then he should be nervous because I wanted to grab him by his suspenders and snap him across the school like a rubber band. Right then I was glad Charlie had taken the gum because I really wanted to give Jeffrey a piece.

Megan and I kept walking. We didn't see the rest of them but I could hear lockers banging and I was glad that my locker was nowhere near theirs. Megan and I were sitting in class when they all showed up. Jeffrey walked across the room and sat down in front of me in his usual seat. I have to say, for the first time ever I had the urge to take my fingers and flick him in the back of the head. I didn't do it, that wouldn't be nice, but I wanted to.

"Deidre, are you chewing gum in my class?" Miss Stanton said loudly, sounding annoyed.

"Yes Ma'am," Deidre answered calmly.

"You know the rules, now spit it out."

"I just had lunch and it cleans my teeth."

"I don't care, spit it out."

Miss Stanton was all about the rules and tried her hardest to make sure that they were followed to the letter. But she was at least nice enough to bring Deidre the garbage can so she didn't have to get up to spit out her gum.

"Okay everyone, quiet down," Miss Stanton said. "Your reports are due today so please take them out and pass them forward. This is not an invitation to talk, please do it quietly."

* * *

Jeffrey was relieved that the teacher had chosen what he considered to be the easiest of his three scenarios for switching the binders. And as his plan went into action he saw Kevin smiling and giving him the thumbs up. Jeffrey's own essay was already on his desk, hidden under two pieces of plain paper. He didn't want to accidently get his report mixed up with the fake Stephen ones in his bag so it was out and ready to go. Jeffrey pretended to be looking through his backpack when he saw the green binder in Stephen's hand, and then he removed the matching colored one from his assortment. When Jeffrey reached back and took Stephen's essay to pass forward, he quickly swapped it for the fake one, putting

Stephen's real one on his lap and covering it with the two pieces of paper that now left his essay uncovered on his desk. The mission was completed as he passed both essays forward to the next student in the row. He turned and gave Devlin and Kevin a head nod. The damage was done. Jeffrey then put Stephen's real essay back into place with the other nine colored folders in his backpack.

Chapter 30

The Smell of Victory

I was relieved to get that essay turned in and off my mind, and with nearly two hours to kill in our last two periods with her, Miss Stanton decided to give the class the rest of the day to study for finals. Now for me this study time was her just giving me permission to go to my happy place and, even though I tried not to, I slipped away.

It was the last inning and the game was pretty much over, but in sports you have to play right to the end. You still have to go up to the plate and play like you're losing by ten, no matter what the actual score is. When I'm at bat I have my usual routine, just like all ball players. I tighten my batting gloves. I give the barrel of the bat a look over and take a couple swings. I step into the box ready to go. The pitcher then goes into his windup and I stay focused on his throwing hand and just keep watching until my eyes pick up the ball. Once I spot the ball I am like a Navy fighter pilot locking on my target. I follow the ball right to the plate and then I explode my arms and hips into the ball and BOOM! The ball comes off the bat and usually flies into the great blue yonder or the parking lot. I start to round the bases and I can see the pitcher talking to himself saying, CRAP! CRAP! Wait, he doesn't say…

"Crap!" Kevin said again.

"Kevin, what did you just say?" Miss Stanton said angrily.

"I need to … awwwww." Kevin grabbed his stomach and moaned.

"What is that smell?" Conner Jenkins yelled out.

Everyone in class was looking around and wrinkling up their noses, trying to figure out where the smell was coming from.

"Miss Stanton I need to go to the nurse," Kevin said. He looked a little green.

Without waiting for an answer, Kevin ran from the class groaning and Miss Stanton walked over to the windows and yanked them all open. The smell in the classroom was bad but had started to clear up a little when a whole new wave came through the room.

"Okay man, that is *not* cool! Who did that?" shouted Eve Strain.

The smell was really awful but of course no one fessed up. A few seconds later, Deidre did go running from the room though. She didn't even ask for permission. Then, right in front of me, I watched as Jeffrey's face began wincing up and the whole room heard what sounded like a balloon when you've blown it up and then let it go, the air hissing back out as it flies around the room. The smell from where I was sitting was unbearable. When Jeffrey stood up a second later there was something black dripping from his pants onto his nice dress shoes.

"Miss Stanton, I have to go to the nurse," Jeffrey said. He looked both shocked and embarrassed.

"Well go, don't just stand there," Miss Stanton ordered.

Jeffrey picked up his backpack and waddled like a duck out of class and down to the nurse's office.

"Okay, now listen up, does anyone else feel sick?" Miss Stanton asked.

Three more hands quickly shot up in the air, including Devlin's.

"Leave your things and go to the nurse. Go now!" Miss Stanton said in a panic. "Everyone else, grab your belongings and follow me."

Chapter 31

A Brilliant Plan

You all have been reading along so you all know that I didn't do this. I didn't. You've been with me this whole time and I gave the gum to Charlie. He told me it was a bad idea and I agreed. You were there when I handed him the gum so this had nothing to do with me. I would have thought maybe food poisoning if it weren't for the fact that the only people it affected were Devlin and the bully gang. "Charlie," I said to myself.

At the end of the day I went to Charlie's locker and waited but he never showed. So I went outside and stood by the buses, waiting for Megan. When the doors came flying open I expected to see her come walking out but instead it was Charlie. He was wearing the biggest *look what I did* grin you have ever seen.

"Charlie," I called out.

"What's up?" he said as he bopped over to me. (Yes, bopped -- he looked like he was dance-walking.)

"What did you do?"

"I didn't do anything."

"Charlie," I said knowingly.

"I didn't." Charlie looked at me and shrugged.

"I'm standing here and it is just you and me."

"Okay, maybe I did do something."

"Charlie, you told me it was a bad idea!"

"I told you it was a bad idea for *you*."

"What's the difference?"

"Stephen, it was a genius idea! How could I not go through with it?"

"What happens when they start putting two and two together and they come up with Charlie?" I asked.

"Well, I'm not sure how they are going to spin it but my guess is they aren't going to say anything."

"Are you crazy? You just made them poop all over the school and you don't think they are going to tell someone?"

"Stephen, I didn't give them the gum."

"What do you mean? You just said you went through with my idea."

"Well I did, but I didn't *give* them the gum."

"So how did they get it?"

"They stole it," Charlie said laughing.

"They stole it?"

"Yes, those idiots stole it." Charlie was still laughing.

"When?" I asked.

"I put the Laxi-Gum into the peppermint packs just like you said you were going to do."

"Charlie." I gave him my best disapproving look.

"What, it was *brilliant*! When you have a brilliant plan in front of you it would be a shame not to use it."

"So how did they steal it?"

"I set the three packs of Laxi-Gum on my lunch tray ..."

"The real Laxi-Gum?" I interrupted.

"Yes, the gum I put in the peppermint packs. It is now on my lunch tray. So I walked over to the table next to Devlin's and set my tray down. Then I asked them to keep an eye on it while I went to get a drink. When I came back those clowns were laughing like little kindergartners."

"What was so funny?"

"Well I guess they thought it was funny to empty all three packs of gum while I was gone."

"What do you mean emptied them?"

"Emptied them. They emptied them. When I came back to the table every single one of them had a wad of my gum in their mouths and the three packs were empty."

"So you didn't actually give them the gum?"

"Nope," Charlie said smiling.

"But you knew once you turned your back they were going to take it."

"I just put the gum out there for them to see, they didn't have to take it."

"But you knew they would."

"Nothing is certain, you know that, but I know them as well as you do so what were my odds?"

"Pretty good."

"Yes indeed," Charlie said as Megan walked up behind us.

"What are you guys up to?" Megan asked.

"Waiting for you," Charlie said with a smile.

"I like vegetables," Megan said curtly. I guess she figured out that this must be Charlie.

"What a waste," Charlie said, frowning.

"Charlie, this is Megan," I said.

"Hi Megan," Charlie was back to smiling again. "Any chance of you rethinking the vegetables?"

"Not a chance, I love them."

"Okay, I guess you're stuck with Stephen then."

"Charlie, the bus," I said, pointing as the bus driver started closing the door.

"Okay, gotta go. Bye, Veggie Girl."

Megan laughed. "Bye, Charlie."

Megan and I stood at the front of the school and waited for the buses to pull out before we started walking. Then she reached over to hold my hand and all I could think was that I could get used to this.

Chapter 32

Megan's Dad

Megan and I sat on the grass with our backs against a tree, watching the water and the colored lights dance in the fountains as Liberace played the piano. Yes, Liberace. I can't tell you why but it works with the water show. I wouldn't listen to him in the car or on my iPod but here, I actually like it. As we were sitting there a big black limousine pulled up the driveway and circled around to the front of Megan's house.

"There's my dad," Megan said, all excited.

She jumped up and grabbed my arm and pulled me along with her. It was a good thing I could stand up quickly because otherwise she would have just dragged me across the lawn. As her dad stepped out of the limo, Megan called out,

"Daddy!"

"Megan," her dad said, sharing her enthusiasm.

Megan let go of me and ran at her dad and then leaped into his arms, knocking him backwards against the car. They both laughed. Then Megan's dad stepped away from the limo, holding Megan the way a parent would carry a small child to bed. I know if I ran at my dad like that he might end up like the catcher I plowed over the other night.

"I missed you," Megan said.

"Me too, Baby," her dad said as he put her down.

Megan's dad was a good looking guy. He was dressed like someone you see in an office, wearing a suit and tie, and his hair was slicked back off of his face. I was looking down at him, so he was shorter than me, but no more than a few inches.

Megan looked at me and said, "Daddy, this is Stephen."

"Hi Stephen, nice to meet you." He reached over and shook my hand. He had a strong firm handshake and I got the impression that he spends some time in the gym.

"You too, Mr. Milton," I said. I looked at him as I shook his hand, trying to make a good impression.

"Megan has been talking a lot about you," he said.

"She has?"

"Yes, she has, and she's right, you do look like Superman." He laughed, but in a nice way.

"She said she told you that but I didn't believe her," I said, feeling a little embarrassed.

"Well, she did. She also told me you are a baseball player?"

"Yes, I am."

"I hear you're good too, is that true?"

"I guess I'm pretty good," I said, making sure not to sound cocky.

"Maybe if I can schedule some time off Megan and I will both come to see you play."

"Really, Daddy?" Megan asked, sounding surprised.

"What? I like baseball, and if he's as good as you say, I'd like to see him play too. You embarrassed to be seen with me now?"

"Never, you know that," said Megan.

"Good, then we'll go." Mr. Milton looked at me. "When is your next game, Stephen?"

"Saturday," I answered.

"Saturday, hmmm," he said, thinking. "I'm not sure about Saturday but we'll see. Megan, I am going to go say hi to Mom and I'll see you inside later. Nice to meet you, Stephen."

"You too, Mr. Milton."

We watched as her dad grabbed something from his car and then walked into the house. His driver started the limo and pulled away.

"Your dad is nice, I like him," I said.

"He is nice, that's my dad!" Megan said proudly.

"Is he serious about coming to one of my games?"

"Yep. If he said he's coming, he's coming."

"Really?" I couldn't believe he was that cool!

"Yes, we both will," Megan said.

"Well then I guess I will have to leave *two* tickets at the gate," I said with a straight face.

And then we both laughed.

Chapter 33

The Perfect Day

If I ever wanted to know what it feels like to have a dream come true then Friday at school was it! From the minute I walked into school I could sense something was different. There was no one hiding around corners calling out mean names as I walked by, no anonymous notes had been slipped into my locker and, like movie magic, the bully gang was gone. Not permanently unfortunately, just for the day, but it was still great. Apparently the entire bully gang had exceeded Laxi-Gum's dosage recommendation and they just could not squeeze school into their very busy bathroom schedules.

I did expect at some point during the day that this great feeling would somehow get ruined. I wasn't sure who would end it but there was a list in my head of possible suspects, with Miss Stanton and Principal Heftler being my top two choices. With the gum issue lingering and questions probably being asked, Principal Heftler was ahead of Miss Stanton by a nose.

But as I sat in history class watching the clock, the second hand tick-ticking away, the final bell rang. I slowly turned around and Megan smiled at me and it was then, and only then, that I experienced what a perfect day really feels like.

Chapter 34

Fans
Yankees VS. Giants

I love Saturday mornings, and where a lot of people take advantage of this day for extra sleep, I am up at the crack of dawn with the roosters. I do lie in bed for an extra few minutes to listen to the sound of the birds making music, but then it's down to business. I get up, use the bathroom, attempt to run a brush through my hair and put on my baseball uniform. I walk down the stairs trying not to make too much noise because my parents are still sleeping. I tiptoe into the kitchen to grab a bowl of Cheerios, a banana and a glass of OJ. Then I move quietly through the living room and out the front door to the porch where I sit in one of the wicker chairs and eat. While I'm eating the sun will peak around the corner of the house and hit my face dead on and I let it. I love how warm it feels and I soak up its energy. And then when I feel my face start to sweat I go back inside. I put my bowl and glass in the sink, grab my hat and cleats and it's time to go.

The baseball fields are less than a mile away if I take the bike path so sometimes I will walk. It's quiet and peaceful out at that time of morning and usually there isn't anyone around. Maybe I'll hear a dog barking or the rumble of a train but the walk is energizing. The air is the coolest it's going to be in the early morning and when you breathe in it almost feels like you've jumped into a pool on a hot day. I walk with my bat thrown over my shoulder and my glove hanging off my bat and as I walk I can hear the rhythm of click, clack, click, clack as my cleats hit the pavement. It sounds like soldiers marching off to war. It's Saturday, and it's time for some baseball!

* * *

"So who are we playing?" Megan said to Charlie.

"We? Not me, I am just here to scout the talent," said Charlie.

"What does *that* mean?" Megan said, looking confused.

"Girls. I'm just here for the girls."

"That's nice, your best friend is playing and you're scouting the talent." Megan smirked at Charlie.

"Trust me, he doesn't need my help."

"We are fans, we ROOT," Megan said, throwing her arms in the air.

"I am a Brave, so Stephen is my competition."

"I heard they beat the Braves 21-2," Megan teased.

"I never said we were *good* competition," Charlie said. "Who's the old guy you came with?"

"That's my dad."

"Why doesn't he come and sit with us?"

"He is giving me my space."

"That's sweet."

"Yes, it is. Now where is Stephen?"

"He's the big guy behind home plate. They call him the catcher."

Megan rolled her eyes. "I know what a catcher is. Are you going to be like this the whole game?"

"I have been like this my whole life."

"Your mother must be proud."

"No, she's Dutch with a little German tossed in."

"Oh my GOSH!" Megan said, then she shook her head.

"What? You have a something against Germans?" Charlie said.

"What? No. Not at all. I have been to Germany and everyone was very nice."

"You have never met my mother."

"Stephen says that your mother is nice."

"Stephen lies. She's like a snapping turtle, all nice and cute and then when you get too close, she bites your fingers off."

"Charlie, that's not nice," Megan said, frowning at him.

"I know it's not, look." Charlie put out his hand, bending two fingers under to show Megan that they were bitten off.

"Stop," Megan said, slapping his hand.

"I see why Stephen likes you, you're feisty." Charlie smiled.

"Are you going to watch the game or just keep talking?"

"I tell you what, once they start the game I'll stop talking."

"Really?"

"Probably not."

Once the game started Charlie chilled out and even started rooting for the Giants. Their competitors today were the Yankees and they were struggling. They had some good pitchers but too many weak fielders. A lot of times in baseball, good pitching can keep you in the game and keep you competitive, but with only two wins this season, the Yankees' pitching wasn't proving to be strong enough.

"Stephen's up," Megan said. She sounded all excited.

"Stephen's up," said Charlie, mocking her, laughing.

Megan looked at Charlie and sneered.

* * *

Normally I love swinging at the first pitch because it is usually a good one. But I also don't want to get a reputation of swinging at the first pitch either because then the pitchers will catch on and I will get junk every time. So today I decided to lay off of it and it flew by me for ball one.

* * *

"Why does he step out of the box after each pitch and tighten his gloves? Are they too big?" Megan asked.

Charlie looked at Megan and rolled his eyes.

"Are you serious?" he said.

"Yes, why does he do that?"

"I thought you said you watch baseball?"

"I do."

"And you never noticed that almost every ball player steps out and tightens their gloves? That's just what they do."

"So they're not loose?"

"No, they are not."

"Then why do it? If they're on right then leave them alone."

"Megan, it is just part of the ritual -- you step out, tighten your gloves, swing your bat -- it's preparing you for the next pitch."

"That seems like such a waste of time."

"Megan, the count on Stephen is three and one. This is going to be the pitch."

"What pitch?"

"Watch."

* * *

There is nothing better for a batter than being up in the count. I can take the pitch or leave it, it doesn't matter. With nothing to worry about I am relaxed, and when I am relaxed, I am really dangerous.

* * *

"Wowww! Did you see him crush that ball!" Charlie had jumped up and was standing, along with most of the other Giants fans.

"I think that's going over the fence," Megan said with

surprise.

"That is not just going over the fence, that is going to take out a windshield. I hope your dad's not parked in the lot."

"Wow! He can hit the ball a long way!" Megan was impressed.

"Megan, if he isn't playing for the Yankees one day, I will eat vegetables," Charlie said, cheering.

* * *

I saw Megan as I rounded third. She was looking at her dad, who was clapping and yelling like every other fan, and she was smiling. Then I caught her eye as I hit home plate and she gave me an even bigger smile. I could tell by her expression that right now, all was good in Megan's world.

The Giants went on to beat the Yankees 12-4, and I went three for five with two stolen bases, a walk, three runs scored and a homer. Not a bad day in my world either.

Chapter 35

Not Fans
Yankees VS. Giants

Devlin and Kevin stood a few feet away from the safety fence that separated the road from the playing field and watched the celebration as strike three was called on Billy Barrett to end the game.

"You have to admit, he's good," Kevin commented.

"I don't have to admit anything," Devlin said, getting angry.

"Chill dude, you don't have to snap my head off."

"Well whose side are you on?"

"I'm with you, you know that."

"It sounded to me like you're his little sissy cheerleader."

"I am not. I just commented, that's all."

"Well don't. You know as well as I do that he had something to do with Thursday. I was on the toilet all night and I even had to miss our game because of the stomach cramps."

"We still won," Kevin said, shrugging.

"That's not the point." Devlin shot him a dirty look.

"I'm not seeing how you're connecting him with the diarrhea."

"He was talking to Brandle just before Brandle sat down next to our table."

"So what? He is always with Brandle."

"I am telling you he did it," Devlin insisted.

"Well we can't prove it, so move on. We have Stephen where we want him anyway. Baseball is his life, and once they take that away from him we'll have the last laugh."

"Jeffrey did do good," Devlin remarked.

"Really good!" said Kevin. "Now can we dump his dweeb butt before we get a bad reputation."

"We can't, not yet."

"Why not?" Kevin protested. "We agreed when the job was done the dweeb would be gone."

"If we dump him now he might get mad and start talking. I think we just let him tag along until the last day of school and then we can ignore him all summer."

"You are kidding, right?"

"No, I'm not kidding."

"He is going to be with us until school is over? That is crazy talk, Dev!"

"Do you want to take the chance of him spilling his guts?" Devlin asked.

"No, but to the end of school?"

"It's got to be that way."

"But to the end of school?" Kevin was pleading.

"Sorry, I don't like it either."

Chapter 36

Still at the Game

Yankees VS. Giants

As soon as the game was over I looked around the fence area and the bleachers to see if I could spot Megan. I had seen her earlier in the game when I hit my home run, so I was hoping to find her waiting for me, but I didn't see her anywhere.

"Stephen," Charlie called out. "Over here! We're over here."

"I don't think he can see us," Megan said.

By now Mr. Martin had joined them in the stands and they were all standing up waving and calling out. I followed the voices calling my name and the first person I spotted was Mr. Martin. Mr. Martin was no longer dressed in his Friday suit and tie and looked much more like an average guy, like us. He had on a pair of blue jeans and a New York Yankees t-shirt, which I thought was cool. His hair wasn't slicked back today, either; it was just hanging down wavy, kind of like Megan's, but a whole lot shorter. He looked much younger today than he did when I saw him get out of the limousine. After a second I saw that Megan was right next to him, smiling and waving, and Charlie was with them too.

"Mr. Martin, hi," I said as I walked over to them.

"Hi Stephen, great game! I am impressed."

"Thank you, sir."

"I was impressed too," said Megan, not wanting to be left out.

"Well that is what's most important," her dad said, laughing.

"Dad." Megan blushed, which I thought was kind of cool.

"Well it's true. He didn't hit that home run for me, I'm sure."

"Dad!"

"I'm just saying."

"Stop," Megan urged.

"Okay, okay."

"We're all going to the Dazz to celebrate," I said to Megan. "Do you want to come with us?"

The Dazz is a place where all of us go for ice cream and burgers after games. It's only a few miles away.

"Dad?" Megan looked at her father to see if he would let her come.

"It's alright with me, but I hope you don't mind if I don't join you. Since I've been away all week I have some things I need to get caught up on at home. You can go, though."

"Are you sure?"

"Yes, Honey, you go and have fun. Do you all need a ride?"

"Thanks, Mr. Martin, but my dad is going to take us," I said.

"Okay, great. If you have it covered, I'm going to run," Mr. Martin said.

"Bye Daddy," Megan said and then gave him a hug.

"Bye, Sweetie."

I watched Megan hug her dad goodbye and could tell how much

she loves him. But what really caught my attention was how Mr. Martin closed his eyes and let his head drop down, almost like he was praying, while he hugged her. I do the same thing when I'm at church so I couldn't help but wonder if he was actually praying. Maybe he was thanking God for that moment, for every new moment He was giving them.

Chapter 37

Jack's in No Mood

My dad's new car was just big enough to get us all buckled into after the game. Jack rode shotgun up front with my dad and in the back was Charlie, me and Megan. My mom had driven her own car to the field because she didn't like the "mayhem" (which is what she called it) that took place at the Dazz after a game, so she went home.

"I don't know why I couldn't go home with Mom," Jack complained.

"Because the whole team is going," my dad said.

"But I just want to go home."

"Come on, Jack, cheer up. We're going to celebrate," Dad said.

"I don't feel like celebrating." Jack was frowning and staring out the side window.

"Jack, baseball is a team sport, we win as a team and we lose as a team. Ask Charlie, he knows," I said.

"Is that a dig?" said Charlie.

"It's a fact. Your team is what, zero and five?"

"No, we are zero and six now, get your facts straight."

"I tell him the same thing all the time," said Jack.

"That's comforting to know. Have we notified Guinness yet?" said Charlie.

"Charlie," I said, smacking him in the shoulder.

"Charlie, that's not helpful," my dad said, but he was smiling.

"Sorry, Mr. Miller."

Megan had no idea what we were talking about so she didn't say anything until now.

"What are you talking about? Why is Charlie sorry?" she asked.

"I'm sorry because I was being insensitive to Jack's strikeout issues," Charlie explained.

"I didn't see Jack strike out," Megan said kindly.

"Remember when you said you had to pee?"

"I never said that." Megan sounded offended.

"Okay, when you said you had to go to the little girl's room. Sorry. But remember I told you if you needed to go that this was the best time to do it?" Charlie said.

"I do remember that."

"That's why you didn't see Jack, you were in the can. I figured you wouldn't miss anything."

"Thanks, Charlie," said Jack.

"Sorry, I didn't mean anything by it," Charlie said.

"But that was only one time. What about the rest of the game? I didn't see him strike out at all," Megan said.

"You went to the snack shack once and then you needed more

sunscreen. He was only up three times."

"I'm sorry, Jack," Megan said, and she seemed to really mean it.

"It's okay," Jack said. And Jack's mood actually seemed to improve after that.

We had no way of knowing for sure if Jack's strikeout streak would continue, but when we got home after the Dazz the phone number for The Guinness Book of World Records was located and written down. It was actually *written down.* I am not kidding, and Jack is the one who went online, researched it and came up with the number. During Jack's research on striking out he discovered that Reggie Jackson, one of the best players to ever put on baseball cleats, held the Major League record in strikeouts. This made Jack much happier, so he wrote down Guinness's number on a little yellow post-it and stuck it right next to the phone. He said if he was going to strike out every single time he batted then something good was going to come out of it. He said, "If Reggie Jackson is good enough for the Guinness Book, so am I."

He promised though that he would not strike out on purpose, just to get the record.

Chapter 38

Trouble's Brewing

When I got to school on Monday the first person I went looking for was Megan. I waited near her locker until the homeroom bell rang but she never showed up. I have to admit I was a little disappointed. I hoped maybe she was just running late, then I'd at least get to see her either during lunch or in Miss Stanton's class. When I got to my homeroom Mrs. Dilts, my teacher, was having a conversation with Miss Stanton and as I went to sit down, Miss Stanton spoke to me.

"Stephen, don't get comfortable, you need to come with me."

"Why?" I asked.

"We need to have a talk, so please come," she said.

Mrs. Dilts nodded her head in my direction, so I followed Miss Stanton out of the room. As we walked down the hall I passed Megan and she started to talk to me but Miss Stanton cut her off.

"Megan, Stephen can't talk to you right now and you need to get to your class. You're late."

Megan gave me this deer in the headlights look and mouthed, "What's going on?" I just shrugged my shoulders and kept walking.

We passed the gym and then the library but we weren't walking in the direction of Miss Stanton's classroom so I didn't know where we were going. But then, as we got near the entrance to the building, the principal came out of the front office into the hallway and motioned to us.

"Miss Stanton, please take Stephen into my office, I will be right in," Mr. Heftler said.

"Yes, Mr. Heftler," said Miss Stanton.

My heart almost stopped beating. I have never been to the principal's office in all the years I've been at school and now, without any warning, I was being led like a prisoner to the gas chamber. Miss Stanton motioned for me to sit and she took the seat right next to me. We both sat facing the principal's desk, waiting. I was glad she didn't say anything to me. Whatever this was about I'd rather hear it from the principal.

Mr. Heftler was a nice little man who enjoyed running, or at least that's what I got from the photos he had scattered around his desk and office. In every picture I could see he was running. One picture was in a frame that said Daddy on top of it. There was a woman and two small kids with him, so I'm thinking it must be his wife and kids, but they were all dressed in running clothes too, so maybe the whole family likes to run. I guess that's kind of cool. Running is a good way to stay thin and Mr. Heftler looked to be in good shape. When he finally walked into the office and shut the door he took a deep breath and exhaled, just like he had been running.

"Okay, let's get down to business," said Mr. Heftler.

Chapter 39

The Bullies Gloat

Of course the whole school was buzzing since a lot of kids had seen Stephen being led around like a dog on a leash by Miss Stanton. Charlie looked concerned when he walked passed them and Megan walked to homeroom worried after Miss Stanton wouldn't let her talk to Stephen. Devlin and the bully gang were all huddled up laughing when they saw him. The only person Stephen walked by who looked like she couldn't care less about what was going on was Peggy Sloan. Her face was almost always serious and what crossed Stephen's mind as he passed her was that Peggy really needed Charlie. She needed someone who could put a smile on her face and put the funny back in her funny bone. Stephen promised himself that it would be his sole purpose in life, if he made it out of his situation, whatever it was, to make sure that Peggy and Charlie united, or at least took in a movie and got to know each other.

"Did you see the look on his face?" Devlin said, laughing.

"I would love to be a fly on the wall to hear what they say," said Deidre.

"I followed them and the principal was waiting for them at the

office," Jenni said as she came racing up the hall.

"It worked, Jeffrey did it," said Kevin, slapping Devlin on the back.

"That kid is toast," said Devlin smugly.

"French!" Kevin replied.

"What are we going to do if he gets suspended for the rest of the year? We won't have anyone to pick on," said Jenni.

"Yeah, who are we going to play with if that happens?" said Debbie, laughing.

"How about his girlfriend?" Devlin said smiling. "There is no reason not to keep it in the family."

"I think that's a great idea," said Kevin.

"I hope we don't make her cry," Debbie said, pretending to wipe her eyes.

"Oh I think we can do better than making her cry," said Kevin.

Chapter 40

The Principal's Involved

I honestly had no idea why Principal Heftler would want to talk to me. The only thing I could think of was the gum incident but I didn't have anything to do with what happened so, even though I was a little nervous, I figured I would survive.

"Stephen, I don't know if you know why you're here, but Miss Stanton came to me with this concern," Mr. Heftler began.

"I'm sorry, Stephen, but we have to address this issue. This type of thing can't be ignored," Miss Stanton said.

"I am a little bit surprised that this has come up, and I hope we can get to the bottom of it," Mr. Heftler said.

"Of what?" I asked, looking back and forth between the two of them. It was like watching a tennis match.

"I don't want to start discussing it until your parents get here. We have some things to go over and paperwork to look at," Mr. Heftler explained.

"My parents are coming?" Now I was panicking.

"Yes, your parents have to be here," said Mr. Heftler.

"What is this about, what papers?" I said.

"Stephen, as Principal Heftler said, we really can't go into all of this without your mom and dad present. They did call to say they'll be a little late, but they're on their way," said Miss Stanton.

"I don't understand, what did I do?"

You could hear the concern in my voice, and not without reason. My parents are coming and the principal is surprised and needs to get to the bottom of something. I have been in this school since kindergarten and I have never been in real trouble so I didn't know what to think now. The only paper I could think of was the Lewis and Clark essay I handed in last week. Suddenly the telephone rang and Mr. Heftler picked up quickly.

"Yes, Nancy? … They're here? … Both of them? … I will have Miss Stanton come out and walk them back. … It's not a problem, we have it covered." Mr. Heftler hung up the phone and looked at Miss Stanton. "They're here. If you could walk them back I would appreciate it."

"Sure," said Miss Stanton, and she left the room.

A few seconds later there was a knock on the door. After the principal said, "Come in," my mom and dad walked in the office. They looked a little worried, which made me more worried. Mr. Heftler stood up and shook their hands and then got right down to business.

"Miss Stanton has brought to my attention something that is very concerning to us and what I would like to do is go over what we have found and talk about how to handle this issue. Just make yourselves comfortable and we'll get started."

Chapter 41

Crime & Punishment

Often we look at things that are right in front of us and we don't see them. Like Jeffrey. He sat in the seat in front of me every day this year and sometimes he would joke with me and we'd laugh. I know that we weren't close friends but out of all the kids to turn on me, Jeffrey hurt the most.

* * *

"You can sit down in those two chairs, it's better if you face me," Miss Stanton said. "Now before you say anything, let me show you what I found and then we can go over the issue and the administrative steps that are going to be taken."

"Administrative steps? Steps for what?" his dad asked.

"For plagiarism," Miss Stanton answered.

"Plagiarism?" his dad asked, shocked.

"Yes, Sir, for plagiarism."

"Plagiarism? Dad, I didn't plagiarize anything, I swear. I didn't."

"Stop talking, Son. Miss Stanton, these are very serious accusations, I hope you have proof."

"I do, unfortunately. If you look at your son's essay, all the sections marked with red have been taken directly out of the text book," said Miss Stanton.

"Okay, now what am I comparing them to?" His dad looked at the papers Miss Stanton was showing them.

"To these," said Miss Stanton, as she handed him five additional pages. "These are photocopies made from the text book and, as you can see, entire sections of text match what your son used in his essay. I have a copy of the text book itself, with each page tabbed, if you would like to read it directly from the book."

"That won't be necessary," his dad said as he examined all of the pages laid on the desk.

"I assure you that this is not easy for me to bring to your attention."

"I am sure it's not."

"Your son has never done anything like this before and it seems completely out of character. I have talked to his teachers all the way down to kindergarten and not one of them had a single bad thing to say about him. But, unfortunately, plagiarism is a serious issue and disciplinary steps have to be taken."

"What kind of steps are you talking about?"

"Suspension, for the remainder of the school year, starting today. He will be allowed back to take his final exams, but those will be taken under close supervision. He will also be required to rewrite his essay, again under supervision, using all his own words this time. This will need to be done after school is out, during the summer school session, and will be required for him to be promoted to eighth grade."

"Anything else?"

"The only other thing is that, since the athletic program in this town is sponsored and paid for by the Board of Education, we are required to notify the sports commission and he will be suspended from all sports activities immediately. He will not be able to attend or participate in any community athletic activities until September."

"Dad, please listen, I didn't do it! I wrote my own paper."

"Stop, Son. It's all right here."

"But Dad, please believe me. Someone must have switched essays!"

"And who would do that?"

He didn't answer. It isn't always good to keep secrets, but sometimes you feel that is what you have to do to survive.

Chapter 42

Talking It Out

The principal went on about how bad he felt and hoped there were no hard feelings, and he assured my parents that we would work through the difficulties. As he talked I just sat looking at the wall, going in and out of my happy place (which was anything *but* happy today), but my mom and dad didn't miss a word. There was a knock on the door and, as it swung open, I realized the meeting was over and my life was about to change. When I got up to leave, Miss Stanton was standing at the door smiling at me. I mean, why not? She did the right thing and she should feel good about it.

"Stephen, get your stuff and we will meet you at the car," Mom said as we all walked out of the principal's office.

"Do you need help?" Dad asked me.

"No, I can get it," I said.

"Let's get going then. We have an appointment at 11:30," Mom said.

"Okay, I'll meet you at the car," I said.

Before I left the building I wanted desperately to talk to Megan and tell her what had happened, but I had very little time. I grabbed

my things and then walked to her locker, thinking it was the one place I might catch her. As I came around the corner, all I saw was Devlin and Kevin talking to Jeffrey, no Megan. I just wanted a minute with her and I get the three stooges instead.

Chapter 43

A Moment of Desperation

Have you ever been so humiliated or so embarrassed that you just want to crawl in a hole and die? In your mind you know how to get out of this mess, the answer is right there in front of you, but whichever decision you make you feel like you're doomed.

The strength that protects each of us from this kind of doom and despair is found within us, but the inner glue that holds each individual together is different. Most days whatever ridicule and name calling there is just rolls off your back. It does hurt, and sometimes it hurts badly, but there are other things in our lives that remove it from our minds for a while. But not today. Today the pain is all consuming.

On the ride home there was nothing positive. There was no understanding, and for the first time, there was no support either. Where was that dad telling you to keep trying, you'll get it, or the mom who lovingly tries to make sure your clothes match so no one will look at you funny? Aren't your parents the ones who are supposed to listen to you and try to uncover the real truth? Kids sometimes lie, we all know that, and once we tell a lie we will stand our ground and protect that lie like it's the last thing we will ever do, but today there was no one even trying to find the truth.

There are two sides to every story and the truth is usually tucked carefully in the middle somewhere. But the truth here was an unknown. Someone had switched papers, that was obvious, but how, and the bigger question, who? And forget about proving it. A conspiracy theory didn't go over well in the meeting because there was no answer for who, and even if there was, in this case, where was the truth really leading? The answer was way too clear.

There was no place to run, there was no place to hide and the truth that would normally set someone free wasn't going to work here. There was nothing but pain, humiliation and embarrassment to the whole family.

The house was quiet at first but the screaming came and wouldn't end. Eventually the phone started to ring as word got around and now came the embarrassing questions that had to be explained to friends and family. But at least when they were on the phone the screaming stopped.

But it wasn't really gone. It kept echoing and bouncing around the bedroom and it wasn't going away. It just kept calling out louder and louder, so loud in fact that it was deafening, and there was no way to make it stop. No one heard the footsteps walking above them because they were too busy explaining away the behavior that put shame on them. They didn't hear the medicine cabinet open or shut because they were too busy wallowing in what had become *their* nightmare. They didn't hear the faucet as the water poured into a cup because they were focused on damage control. They didn't hear the voice at the top of the stairs say goodbye because they just couldn't hear.

Chapter 44

A Cry for Help

In a small town nothing stays secret for long, so when a siren goes off, it's like a sonic boom, and everyone is quick to pick up their phones to find out why. There are numerous people in Lamington who are elderly or who suffer with aliments that might threaten their lives, but when people started to hear who this siren was for, the gasps could be heard as loud as the siren itself.

The first one to respond to the 911 call was Officer David Porcelli. He quickly examined the scene and was doing CPR when the EMTs arrived.

"David, what have we got?" Stan, one of the EMTs, asked.

"Possible overdose," Officer Porcelli replied.

Stan is a Lamington EMT and has been a resident of town for many years. He is not only an EMT and a volunteer fireman but he is the head of the Lamington Athletic Commission, so he knows most the kids in town pretty well.

"Is he alive?" Stan asked.

"Yes, I just got a pulse, but he wasn't breathing when I arrived," Officer Porcelli explained.

"Do you know how long he's been down?" Stan and the other EMTs assumed control and began evaluating the boy's condition.

"The father said they had been home only a few hours but the parents were on the phone so they don't know exactly."

"What did he take?"

"The mom said sleeping pills and antidepressants. I have the bottles."

"How many pills?"

"She doesn't know exactly, but one was refilled last week and the other one is due to be refilled in four days."

"Thirty day scrips?"

"Yes, on both of them."

"Okay we'll take it from here. Good job, David."

"I hope he makes it. Do you know him?"

Stan nodded his head and said, "Yes."

When the EMTs finally wheeled the gurney from the house a crowd had gathered in the street and on their lawns. The common feeling in town was of disbelief. The siren screamed *get out of the way* and the ambulance was gone in a flash. It was only minutes down the road when the EMTs were sent into full resuscitation mode; the monitor flat-lined and their patient went into cardiac arrest. The voices inside the vehicle were calm but urgent at the same time. All the right measures were taken to bring life back, to zap it back before it was too late. Stan fought for this life, he knew this life and so badly wanted to save it, but at 3:30pm the vehicle slowed down and the emergency lights flickered off.

Chapter 45

Good Intentions Gone Bad

By early evening everyone in Lamington had heard the sad news and tears were in abundance, as were the feelings of guilt and regret.

Mr. Heftler sat in his living room dressed in his running clothes just staring at his TV. It didn't matter what was on, he wasn't watching it anyway. He was brokenhearted and wanted to make some sense of this tragedy. The most troubling thing for him was the nagging feeling that he should have done something differently. Did the punishment fit the crime, because it surely didn't fit the outcome.

Miss Stanton, who often came across as hard and heartless, was so distraught that she checked herself into a private medical facility for observation. She would stay there for a few days while she came to terms with her actions and her part in this terrible loss.

Devlin and Kevin were playing basketball after school when Devlin received a text from Jenni. After they saw the message they stood there for a minute in shock. Then Devlin put his phone back down and they went back to their game.

All the people who loved him and had watched him grow were all trying to come to terms with this loss. Even Stan, whose interaction had been so limited, went home and hugged both of his children like it was the last time.

There was only one person in Lamington who understood the same pain and the same desperation that led to this act, and that was Megan. Megan Milton, the poor girl who had chosen the same path only with far different results. Her reaction was one of simple devastation. She had fought her own battle, pushed away her own demons and sadness. Megan was still angry with herself for what she had done and for the pain and grief she had caused her parents, but that would continue to fade with time. She had lived through the worst of it to find there was happiness in the future, and that future, as it turned out, wasn't that far away; in fact, only a few months. Her smile had returned and she felt hopeful, but now she was heartbroken and in pain once again.

Chapter 46

A Sad Day to Play

Giants VS. Red Soxs

Despite all the tragedy in the world, the sun will still rise. Each day moves forward minute by minute and then resets itself at the end to start a new one. Time doesn't stop to pay its respect; it doesn't pause to pay tribute to those who have left us. It just moves on, and so do the lives of everyone still here.

At the little league game the following night, both teams stood along the foul lines in front of their dugouts while the National Anthem played. Pastor Taylor came out at the end and said a short prayer and everyone in attendance bowed their heads and observed a moment of silence afterward.

When the game was called to action and all the players had taken their positions not a single boy from either team was in the mood to play baseball. The Giants played their worst game of the year, losing to the Red Sox for their second loss of the season. The one and only run scored was on a passed ball, but no one seemed to care. It's fair to say that the only people who paid attention to the final score -- Giants 0, Red Sox 1 -- were the coaches who had to put it in the books.

Chapter 47

Paying Their Respects

Just because the world moves on doesn't mean this tragedy was now forgotten. It was still very much on everyone's mind. The viewing was held at Stafler's Funeral Home, where the turnout was as large as expected. It was also as sad as expected. People hugged and cried and the question that was still circulating was, "Why?" Why would someone with such a bright future take it all away? Most people eventually come to terms with accidents and tragedies that are out of their control, but no one can ever quite accept the reality of someone doing it on their own.

Megan came with her mom and dad but said her goodbyes from a distance. She couldn't bring herself to go up to the coffin. Charlie and Jack have both always said that they couldn't bear to see dead bodies up close and personal -- the one time each of them had, they both had nightmares for weeks -- but this time they both felt they needed to.

Everyone from their community came to pay their respects but, by the end of the day, the lines grew small and everyone in town had said their goodbyes.

Chapter 48

The Service

Neither Jack nor Charlie have ever understood the concept of what is or is not appropriate, but in times of death people come to terms with grief in different ways. So, while it might not have been appropriate for Jack and Charlie to be talking while the memorial service was going on, no one around them seemed to hold it against them. But if you had heard what they were talking about and were totally offended and wanted to tell them to shut up, that would have been an acceptable response too. Everyone's reactions are different at times like this, you can't take it personally.

That being said, Charlie and Jack's possibly inappropriate debate was over fire or dirt. It is a concept they had never given much thought to until now, but the sermon made them think about it. If you had to make this decision, what would it be, fire or dirt?

"No one is sticking *me* into a fire," Jack said sounding angered.

"I can't believe they went that way," Charlie said, "although, maybe the thinking here was how cold it would be to be stuck underground forever."

"He's dead, he can't feel it."

"I know, but it does get cold and the space is so small and cramped. I'd get claustrophobic."

"I think you are missing the point Charlie, you'd be dead."

"No, I get the point, but I do get claustrophobic so maybe fire is the better option for me," Charlie pointed out. "Jack, aren't you afraid of the dark?"

"Who told you that?" Jack sounded surprised.

"Stephen did. He once told me you have a Snoopy nightlight. Was he telling the truth?"

"That was years ago."

"So what is it now?" Charlie teased.

"Spiderman," said Jack.

"So he was telling the truth, you are afraid of the dark? I think you'd be better off with the fire option too."

"Stop! I am not afraid of the dark, it's just easier to see when I get up to use the bathroom."

"So you get up a lot at night to go to the bathroom? That sounds like it could be a serious problem."

"It's not a problem," said Jack.

"It sounds like a problem," Charlie insisted.

"It's not."

"Have you seen a doctor?"

"Will you stop, I don't get up *that* often."

"How often?" asked Charlie.

"Not very."

"What does that mean? Once, twice, three times?"

"I usually sleep through the night," Jack answered.

"So then you really aren't using the light to go pee."

"I am too."

"That's what you're saying, but I don't see any peeing going on. What you're really doing is just wasting electricity. Save your mom and dad some money and get rid of the nightlight."

"I don't want to," Jack said.

"So you *are* afraid of the dark?"

"I am not!"

"So why not get rid of the light in your room? I know there's one in your hallway near the bathroom, so why have the one in your room?" Charlie was not letting this go.

"I just told you why."

"Yeah, you're afraid of the dark, that's why."

"I am not," Jack said again.

"Okay, for your sake let's just say you're not afraid. Now, just imagine you're in the coffin and suddenly you wake up and it's pitch black, what is running through your mind?"

"Nothing is running through my mind."

"That's a given, but let's just say you have a mind that something can run through, dead or alive. What are you thinking?"

"I am thinking that you are an idiot just like my brother said."

Jack and Charlie made very little headway in their debate over fire versus dirt, but it did manage to keep them both from thinking too deeply about why they were really here. For everyone else, the service was moving, though not excessively somber, and the pastor had some very thought provoking things to say. But when all is said and done, words can never fill in the holes that are left behind.

Chapter 49

Missing Stephen

Megan had not been in school since Monday and her first day back on Thursday was a tough one. The past few days were weighing on her mind and it was hard for her to stay focused. This was one of Stephen's biggest problems in school and for the first time she understood how hard it was to learn like that. Megan found herself thinking of him a lot and when she did she caught herself smiling. She wanted to see him so bad, she just wanted to run out of the classroom and find him, but she knew she couldn't. The good news about Megan's concentration problem was that it wasn't a daily issue for her. Also, since it was the end of the school year, Miss Stanton and all the other teachers were only reviewing material that she already knew so she wasn't really missing anything anyway.

When the final bell of the day rang Megan was ready to go home. Today had seemed exceptionally long and she felt drained from the stress of the past few days. She was standing at her locker, just about to shut it, when a hand grabbed the top of it and stopped her.

"Hey, where are you going?" asked Kevin, holding on to her locker.

"Home," Megan replied. "Now please let go."

"Why are you in such a rush?"

"Because I want to go home and I need to catch the bus, that's why."

"I could walk you home," Kevin said, touching her arm.

"Don't touch me." Megan pulled her arm away.

"I just thought I could get to know you better."

"I don't want to get to know you better."

"Why not?"

"Because I don't. I'm not interested and I don't have to explain why to you. Now please, leave me alone."

"Oh, come on," Kevin said, now touching her shoulder.

"No, and I told you to stop touching me." Megan said this with force, but her face gave away that she was getting nervous.

"What's the matter, Megan, I'm not hurting you," Kevin persisted.

"I said, stop!" Megan pushed his hand off of her and took a step back.

"Let me at least walk you home?"

"No."

"You let that moron walk you home but not me?" Kevin was starting to sound angry. He took a step closer to Megan.

"Kevin, I think you better leave before you get hurt," Megan said, looking and sounding more confident.

"And who is going to hurt me, you?" Kevin laughed.

"No, not me."

"Then who?"

"How about me, Kevin?"

Kevin turned around as I was dropping my backpack onto the floor behind him.

"Hey, Stephen, what's up?" Kevin said, his voice sounding a little panicked.

"I don't know, what's up, Moron?" I answered.

* * *

Okay, I know you're thinking, "Where did *he* come from?" Let me finish with Kevin and then you'll understand better.

* * *

"Dude, that was just a figure of speech. I didn't mean anything by it."

"Really?" I tried to keep my eyes locked on his, to scare him a little, but he quickly looked down.

"Yeah, really."

"So what are you doing, Kevin?"

"I just thought that Megan needed some help with her locker is all."

I looked away from Kevin for a second.

"Hi Megan," I said, smiling at her.

"Hi, nice to see you," Megan said back.

"You too! Are we doing nothing today?" I asked her.

"I was thinking we might want to think about doing *something*. I'm getting a little tired of nothing, aren't you?"

"I think you might be right," I said. Then I turned back to Kevin, who was looking really uncomfortable, before asking, "Did you need help with your locker, Megan?"

"Not really," she answered.

"So Kevin isn't really helping much is he?"

"No he isn't."

"Wow, Kevin, it doesn't sound like Megan needs your help."

"Welllll ..." said Kevin, stammering.

"As a matter of fact, I believe I heard her tell you to leave her alone and what did you do?"

"I was going to leave her alone," Kevin said.

"When? Before or after you put your hands on her and told her you …, wait. I can't remember exactly what you said because I'm a moron. Megan, help me here, what did he say?"

I was having fun watching Kevin squirm. He wasn't his usual confident self without support from the bully gang.

"He wants to get to know me better," said Megan

"He didn't say that, did he?" I asked with fake surprise.

"He did." Megan seemed to be enjoying this as much as I was.

"Stephen, come on! I was only kidding around." Kevin's voice sounded almost pleading.

"You think that is kidding around?"

"Yeah, just a joke."

"Megan, did you find it funny?" I asked.

"No," she said matter-of-factly.

"On a scale from one to ten with ten being a belly laugh, where was he on your funny meter?"

"Zero."

"See Kevin? Megan didn't find it funny."

"Well sometimes I miss, it happens," said Kevin.

"Have you ever seen me play baseball?" I asked.

"Yeah, why?"

"I don't miss."

As I took a step closer to Kevin I saw the fear in his eyes. I wasn't proud of what I was about to do, but I needed to stop them in their tracks. I couldn't let the bully gang think that Megan could be their next victim. It just couldn't happen. In the back of my mind was everything my dad said about diplomacy, about doing everything possible to avoid violence. I know he's right, but I just couldn't let them start bullying someone else. Especially not Megan.

Chapter 50

Finishing Up With Kevin

At this point I can only imagine what you're thinking, but let me tell you that June 17th might be the best day of my life. It's not because I put Kevin down with three punches because I didn't, even though that's what I wanted to do. It was because I stood up to the bully gang for once in my life and finally said *stop*.

It's funny how those lessons your parents teach you on right and wrong have a way of controlling your behavior even when your parents aren't around. As much as I thought I was going to knock Kevin out, right there in front of Megan's locker, my dad's words won out. What I did have fun doing was grabbing Kevin by his shirt and dragging him down the hall, kicking and screaming, to the front office. It was also fun to see the look on the secretary's face when I dropped him down right in front of Mr. Heftler.

The look on Mr. Heftler's face was one of complete shock and I'm not sure he was happy with me, but when Megan was done telling him what had happened at her locker he understood. Kevin was in trouble, and just when I thought it couldn't get any better, Megan called her dad and he came in and filed an official complaint against Kevin. A policeman came to the school and Kevin's dad and my dad had to come in so he could talk to each of us about what happened. It all took a long time but it was worth it to see Kevin finally get in trouble for his actions.

I don't know if you know this, because I didn't, but if someone just touches you or you tell someone to leave you alone when they touch you it can be considered criminal battery. They don't have to punch you or push you, they just have to touch you in a way that makes you feel threatened. Now you didn't see the look on Megan's face when Kevin was touching her but I did. She looked scared. And now Kevin was going to be punished.

Chapter 51

The Tale of Megan's Locker

I don't know if you've been keeping track, but I have gone to Megan's locker looking for her a bunch of times. And in all those times, how many times have I found her? The answer is zero. I know you're thinking that's not right, it was twice counting today, but I wasn't really looking for her either of those two times. The first time I just ran into her. And today, well, I sort of ran into her again. The strange thing is the locker Megan was at today was not the same locker she was at the first time. In fact, the first locker was actually two hallways away from where I ran into her today so which one's her locker? Aren't you curious? I know I am.

Megan and I had a full afternoon of doing something after all. It included wrestling Kevin down the hallway, a trip to the principal's office and a lesson on criminal law from the policeman who came to file Mr. Martin's complaint against Kevin. After we were done at the school, Megan asked her dad if I could come over for a bit. Mr. Martin and my dad both said it would be okay, so I went home with the Martins. Megan and I sat down on one of the benches and watched the water show, which seemed normal, but I could tell something was bothering her and I hoped it wasn't something that I did.

"Can I ask you something?" I said.

"It depends what it is. Is it personal?" Megan asked.

"It's about your locker."

It was like I pushed a button. Her eyes suddenly filled with tears and again I didn't know what to do.

"What did I say?" I asked.

"Nothing." Megan stared at the fountains.

"Then why are you crying?"

"Stephen, I need to tell you something." She turned and looked at me.

"What?"

"It has to do with the locker."

"Okay."

"When I first started school here they assigned me a locker and when I went to put my things away it was already being used."

"Yeah?"

"I had just opened it and this kid dressed in a suit and tie started to yell at me."

"Jeffrey?"

"Yes, Jeffrey. He just went off on me, yelling about his right to privacy and breaking and entering. I tried to explain that I was new, that I didn't know it was someone's locker, but he didn't want hear it so I walked away and went back to the office."

"What happened when you went to the office?" I asked.

"They said it was their mistake, they gave me the wrong locker number, and then they gave me another one."

"So where is your locker?"

"My locker is the one you saw me at today."

"So you were in Jeffrey's locker that day? Why?"

"After you left my house the other day I started thinking about them sending you things in the mail and it reminded me of the day I opened his locker. He got awfully mad over nothing. So a couple of days later I was walking by his locker and for kicks I thought I would try and open it again. I didn't even know if I would remember the combination but I did."

"That's pretty good!" I was impressed.

"I have a good memory. But anyway, I opened the door and he had all kinds of magazines and books stacked up, which I didn't bother with, but then I noticed this stack of folders on the top shelf. He had eleven essay folders, I counted them. He had to have every color they sell with only one duplicate."

"What color was that?"

"Black."

"Black's not really a color you know." I had learned that in art.

"Stephen." Megan's voice was firm.

"I'm just saying."

"Can I continue?"

"Sorry."

"Anyway, I was curious about the folders so I pulled them down and your name was on every single one of them, except the last one, which was the extra black one. That one had Jeffrey's name on it."

"He had essays with my name on them?"

"Yes, and what I noticed flipping through them was that they were all exactly the same."

"Really?" I was completely confused.

"Yes," Megan said. "These essays also had tons of mistakes and didn't follow any of Miss Stanton's guidelines. If Miss Stanton were to grade any one of them you would have failed."

"All of them were supposed to be mine? And they were all bad?"

"All but the last one in the black folder, that one had Jeffrey's name on it and it was perfect."

"Why didn't you come and tell me?"

"Because I thought it would be funny to get him in trouble and I didn't want you involved."

"In trouble how?"

"I figured I would give him a taste of his own medicine and do to him what it looked like he was going to do to you. So I switched the one essay that had Jeffrey's name on it with the one in the green binder that had yours."

"Green's my favorite color," I said.

"I know, that's why I picked it."

"So, you switched the folders so he'd fail?"

"Yes."

"But how do you know that's what he was going to do?"

"Stephen, he had ten fake essays in ten different colored folders and they all had your name on them. What else would he

be doing with those? I couldn't know for sure, but the chances looked pretty good that he was going to set you up to fail."

"So you thought somehow he was going to switch my essay for one of the fake ones?"

"Yes, that's what I thought."

"So if you switched essays and he switched essays whose essay does Miss Stanton have?"

"She has yours."

"How is that possible? My essay was in my locker."

"Toni."

"What about Toni?"

"Toni had your locker last year."

"So?"

"The school doesn't change the locker combinations each year. I guess there are so many lockers they can't be bothered doing it."

"How do you know this?"

"Toni told me a few weeks ago, and to prove it she opened your locker."

"You guys were in my locker?"

"She didn't go in it, she just opened it. *I* went in your locker," Megan explained.

"You know that is a violation of privacy?"

"I am aware, can I finish?"

"Yes."

"I told Toni I had a surprise for you so she gave me the combination."

"Well, this is all a surprise."

Megan looked at me. “Stephen, this is hard enough, can you please stop interrupting me?”

“Sorry,” I said, “this is all just very surprising.”

“I know.” She took a deep breath. “So I took your essay to the library and copied it. Yours also happened to be in a green binder, I want to point out. When I finished, I put yours back in your locker. Then I went back to Jeffrey’s locker and switched the essay in his green binder with the one you wrote so Miss Stanton would have the real one if he did switch it.”

“You do realize by switching it back to my own essay that I will probably fail anyway.”

“Sorry,” Megan said, “but at least you will have failed it on your own.”

“That’s comforting.”

“Stephen, they didn’t just want you to fail that paper. A lot of it was plagiarized, which is why Jeffrey got suspended from school.”

“I know.”

“But that was supposed to be you!”

“I know, and you saved me, so why do you look sad?”

“I got Jeffrey killed,” Megan said, her eyes filling again with tears.

“No you didn’t,” I assured her. “Jeffrey got Jeffrey killed.”

“But if I had just told the teacher what he was doing then he might still be alive.”

“Jeffrey could have told them the truth himself, when he got caught, and he didn’t. Why do you think that is?”

"I don't really know," said Megan.

"What do you think the school would have done with that information?"

"He would have gotten into trouble."

"Yes, and maybe worse trouble than he was already in, and then he also had Devlin and the bully gang to deal with."

"That's true."

"I even saw Kevin and Devlin with him at his locker the day he got suspended, they must have been trying to figure out what was going on."

"Do you think?"

"Thinking about it now, yes, that had to be what happened. Devlin and Kevin must have heard that Jeffrey had met with Miss Stanton and wanted to know what he had told her."

"What makes you think that?" asked Megan.

"I don't know why I didn't think about this before, but on the day my parents and I met with Mr. Heftler about me being tested for Attention Deficit Disorder, Miss Stanton had left to get my parents but she never came back in the room. It wasn't until the very end when she knocked on the door to see how things were going that I saw her again."

"So you think she was meeting with Jeffrey's parents?"

"She must have been. It's funny the things you see that you don't really pay attention to, because now I remember seeing Jeffrey with his parents as we were saying goodbye to Mr. Heftler."

"You saw them in the office?"

"Yes, I saw them leaving, but then I saw Jeffrey again right after that at his locker and everything seemed normal."

"But it wasn't, and I feel terrible," Megan said.

"But there was nothing you could have done. He felt trapped with no way out, isn't that how you told me you felt in Connecticut?"

"Yes."

"I want to tell you something."

"What?"

"The pooping thing in class the other day was my idea," I confessed.

"Stephen!"

"I didn't actually have anything to do with what happened, but the plan was mine. I bought the Laxi-Gum when I went to the store with my mom the other night."

"You bought that kind of gum in front of your mom?"

"Yeah, right. NO! When my mom and I left the store, I told her I forgot something and went back and bought it. I couldn't buy it in front of her. How would I explain why I needed Laxi-Gum?"

"You couldn't."

"No I couldn't, but my plan was to go to school the next day and share it with Devlin and the rest of them."

Megan looked at me funny. "Stephen, where did you get that idea from?"

"I got it from something that Charlie did."

"What did he do that would give you such an idea?"

"I promised not to tell anyone."

"You won't tell me? I just told you about switching the essays," Megan said, sounding hurt.

"I'm sorry. I would tell you, but I'd feel bad because I promised Charlie I wouldn't tell anyone."

"Stephen." Megan's eyes were pleading with me.

"Let me think about," I said, feeling bad.

"Really, you have to think about?"

"Let me finish this first and then I'll tell you."

"Okay."

"Anyway, it was Charlie who talked me out of it doing it. He told me what a bad idea it was and how I would get in trouble and not to do it."

"And?"

"I didn't do it. I gave Charlie the gum and went to class."

"So Charlie did it?"

"Not directly. Charlie just left his lunch try on the table next to the bully gang, with the gum on the tray, and asked Devlin to watch it. When he came back they had taken all of his gum and left the empty wrappers on his tray."

"They stole his gum?"

"Isn't that funny? They stole his gum." Even after everything that's happened, thinking of this was still funny.

"So nobody really gave it to them, they did it to themselves."

"Exactly, just like Jeffrey. No one forced him to do what he did either. It was his decision that got him into trouble, you just caught him at it, that's all."

"But Devlin, Kevin and the rest of them get a free pass like it never happened. It's not fair."

We both sat there for a second, staring at the fountains.

"No," I said finally, "it isn't."

Chapter 52

A Close Call

Mets VS. Giants

The evening was filled with dark clouds and light rain. The coaches had their work cut out for them as they kept trying to keep the baseballs dry for their pitchers.

My first at bat resulted in a ground ball to the shortstop, but he misfired the throw, sending the wet ball over the first baseman's head, letting me get to second. I advanced to third base on a ground ball to first, and then scored on a ball thrown in the dirt that rolled right past the catcher.

Jack came to the plate in the third inning and swung at two pitches over his head for the first two strikes, then he stepped out of the batter's box calling time as he adjusted his gloves. I had to laugh watching him do this because he has been playing baseball his whole life and has never before stepped out to adjust his gloves. I think Jack has been watching a little too much of the Yankees on TV. He settled back into the box and you could see him eyeing up the pitcher. The pitch came in just the way Jack likes them, high and fast, and I thought for a second about the World Record Book number next to the phone. Jack waited on the pitch and, as expected, hacked away at it like a lumberjack. But for the first time this season his bat made contact. Jack was in shock and had to be reminded to run as we all screamed at him. Everyone watched the ball as it headed down the line in the direction of the right field fence. We were all screaming *go, go, go* and just as it looked like it was going to clear the fence for a home run, the ball nailed the top about six inches to the right of the foul pole.

"Foul ball," the umpire called out.

Every fan in the bleachers moaned, including the ones for the Mets team. Everyone there was rooting for Jack. We all knew he wanted a hit more than anything in the world and he almost had it. Unfortunately for Jack, that may have ended up being the hit that got away. Jack picked up his bat angrier now than I had ever seen him and I could tell that he was crying. How could you not feel bad for him? He stepped back into the batter's box all teary eyed and recorded his twenty-second strikeout of the season on the same exact pitch. At the end of the night it was Mets 3, Giants 9, and Jack 0 for 3 (again).

Chapter 53

Wrong is Wrong

I went home after the game and was feeling good and bad at the same time. I had a great night so I should be flying high. I tripled, doubled and then they walked me in the sixth. I did luck out with the shortstop's bad throw to first, but that's baseball. What was weighing me down was all the other stuff: Jack's missed hit, Megan's locker visit from Kevin, and Jeffrey. I couldn't stop thinking.

After laying in bed for thirty minutes I realized that I was not going to fall asleep, so I flipped on the light next to my bed and sat up. The first thing I noticed when the light came on was my trophy wall and then, without fail, I started thinking about baseball which, in turn, got me thinking about Devlin.

It was hard to for me to understand how Devlin and his little band of bullies got to walk through life crushing people with no concern about consequences. Megan said it today, it's just wrong, and she's right. I know it and they certainly have to know it, but they just don't care.

I got out of bed, walked over to my closet and pulled the door open. I knew what I was looking for but had to move a few things out of the way to find it. When I did, I sat down on my bed to empty its contents out. My mom likes for us to keep a year-to-year school folder. Both Jack and I each have our own and the binders contain things that happen to us during each school year. Every page has a class photo for that school year and my mom prints the year by hand nicely above it on the binder's page. The folder is filled with school records like report cards and the Presidential Fitness Awards, photos from parties and sports events. I even have my late slips from times I went to the doctor or dentist. I keep everything. I like having mementos to help remember each school year.

I emptied one of the folder sections onto the bed and looked through the pile. I unfolded an old report card and looked at all the D's and wondered if that would all now change.

I have ADD, it was now officially diagnosed. I have been struggling with this for so many years and I finally know what it is. I knew I wasn't lazy and I wanted to say, "See Mom, it has nothing to do with trying harder," but I didn't. When we met with Miss Stanton and Mr. Heftler that day I think both of my parents were relieved that this is something real. It's something we can work with and try to make better. How much better? Well, that is yet to be determined, but at least now I have some hope.

I like the abbreviation ADD better than the actual name of it. Attention Deficit Disorder sounds a little scary. It even sounds creepier when I say it slowly in my scary voice, *Attention - Deficit - Disorder*. The doctor said ADD can affect a lot of things, but for me it's the inability to concentrate and stay focused. I always thought this was going to block so many roads for me in my life, but maybe not now.

Mr. Heftler wasted no time putting together a plan. He said it was just something to start with and that he would be meeting with the school specialists to firm up how things will work for me going forward, but his temporary plan went into action at school today. For now I will be pulled from classes for extra help so I can try to pass the last two exams I have coming up. Any subjects I end up failing this year I will get extra help with in summer school. Today I worked with the math specialist.

I looked at one of my class photos, where all the students are pictured together. I looked at each face slowly and was surprised that each one made me feel something different. Every person's face came with memories, both good and bad, but what really struck me is that there are so many other kids just like me. The kids who don't fit into the cookie cutter cool mold for whatever reason. A lot of those kids had also been hurt by bullies, and maybe it was Devlin or maybe, like with Jack, it was the Sullivan boys. It doesn't really matter who is doing the bullying, it's being done and it is wrong.

Chapter 54

Speak Up and Be Heard

The nagging question for me has always been how can something so obvious not be seen? I know I've mentioned this before, so how? The kids all know who's getting bullied, just like we all know who's doing the bullying (or at least most of them). No one says anything, for whatever reason, but we kids see what is going on. But if you ask any of the adults in our lives, whether it's teachers or parents or coaches, they might come up with one or two situations that really stand out but that's it. Why don't they see it? I have asked myself this question a million times. WHY? Can it be because they don't really participate in our everyday world? Maybe it's because they are busy correcting papers and making class plans or thinking about their lives and families. Kids live in a kid's world and adults do not so maybe it's just not as obvious as I once thought. So after everything that's happened here lately, I'm thinking that if it is not obvious to them, it's time to put it out there for them to see, like the lighted sign at The Dipper.

I went to Megan first with my plan and I explained what I want to do. It doesn't need to involve her -- I know if she comes forward

with what she did that people might get mad at her -- but I want her to know about it before I do anything. When she said she wants to help I wasn't surprised, but I did try to talk her out of it.

"Megan are you sure you want to do this, because I can do it all on my own."

"I have to do this," she said.

"You're probably going to get in trouble."

"I know, but I want to do this. I just do."

"Are you sure?"

"Yes."

"Okay, we'll do it together," I said.

"Together," Megan said.

The next step was to talk to our parents. Megan and I sat down with my mom and dad first and I spilled my guts. My dad has said they want to know what is going on in my life so I told them everything. I even had the evidence to prove it all.

Over the years I had saved every nasty note and item that was ever sent my way and they were all safely put away in my closet. I showed my parents the CDs, flower seeds and all the notes, and then Megan and I worked our way into the Jeffrey story.

My parents received all this information registering both anger (not at me of course, but at the other kids) and disbelief. They both said they were also saddened by everything we were telling them and wondered out loud how I could have let this go on for so long. My dad asked why I hadn't come to them for help and all I could really come up with was I didn't want to make it worse.

Megan's dad and mom didn't take the news well at all. They

were horrified and very angry. They couldn't believe they had moved to get away from this and here it was again. They were mad at Megan for what she had done but still supportive. Mr. Martin said that Megan's choice to switch papers on Jeffrey was the wrong one but he agreed that Jeffrey's punishment would likely have been the same, if not worse, if she had just gone to the teacher. He also commented that what happened with Kevin made a lot more sense now that they knew the whole story.

My parents met with Megan's parents to discuss the options and how they should move forward. Their biggest concern is actually Jeffrey's parents. We're all aware of the grief the Talins are experiencing and everyone thinks throwing this at them right now might be terribly insensitive. But it's clear that something has to be done. The big question is what?

Mr. Milton contacted his attorney to make sure Megan is clear of any legal wrong doing. The lawyer said that Megan switching the papers is not punishable by law but it might be punishable by the school. He said we should argue that Megan really only switched Jeffrey's essay with another essay he had also written and that the intent of her actions should only get her a slap on the wrist or a good talking to. The entering of Jeffrey's locker is a different story but one he feels needs to be discussed with the school.

Chapter 55

Head Case

Giants VS. Orioles

Baseball is no different than any other sport; the people playing the game have to maintain a level of focus and intensity to drive them through a game. But even the greatest athletes have those days where they can't keep that focus throughout the event. It doesn't have to be a total focus meltdown, it can be just a few little thoughts that pop into your mind at the wrong times.

Like today, I am standing at the plate and I have worked the pitcher into a full count and now I'm just dug in waiting for the gravy pitch. I know he has to throw me a strike, I know it's coming, but as I'm watching the ball in his hand, Mr. Heftler pops into my mind. I try to push him out and refocus but by the time I do it, I'm watching strike three whiz by me. My perfect pitch was there and gone.

"Batter's out," I hear the umpire call.

Now I am left standing at the plate, shaking my head in disgust. Embarrassed, I tuck my tail between my legs and head back to the dugout.

In the fourth inning I get a long hit that bounces off the fence

and right back to the left fielder, leaving me with just a single. I took a short lead at first and waited on the pitcher. The pitcher threw over a few times to keep me honest but I had the go sign from my coach and I was getting ready to bolt. I was watching the pitcher's legs and then it happened again -- Mr. Heftler popping in to say hi. I shook my head, physically trying to shake the thought loose, but when it vanished, the first baseman was already holding the ball. The only choice I had at that point was to run, and by the time the perfectly executed pickle play was done, I was called out and on my way back to the dugout.

I held it together in the seventh when I tripled off of the Orioles' relief pitcher and then scored on a single up the center. But with the exception of that at bat, my night was filled with outside interruptions. We did go on to beat the Orioles 5-4, but with my head in the clouds for most of the game, it could have gone either way.

Chapter 56

Mr. Heftler's Taking Over

A meeting was set up with Mr. Heftler to go over all the details and present the evidence. Both Megan's and my parents were there, and the Miltons' lawyer came to go over the issue of Megan entering the locker without permission. Mr. Heftler sat and listened carefully and looked at everything I brought in and he didn't really let on how he felt one way or the other until it was all out in the open.

When we were done explaining everything Mr. Heftler said he wished I had come forward sooner. He said he could have taken the proper steps to stop the behavior from continuing. You could see in his face and tell from the way he spoke that he was deeply bothered by all of this and he said many times how awful he felt for me. He said he knew from experience how I must feel.

I have to admit that when I look at an adult I never think of what it was like for them as a kid, but it was a good feeling to know Mr. Heftler understood what I've been going through. I tried to imagine someone trying to stuff him into a locker as a kid. I actually think even now he would fit -- all the running has kept him pretty thin and I think he would slip right in.

By the afternoon, Mr. Heftler had contacted all the parents of the kids named in our complaint and scheduled a meeting for the next morning at 7:30am. It was a half day and the last day of the school year, but Mr. Heftler wanted the issue addressed now, before summer vacation officially starts. Most of the parents were not thrilled with the suddenness of the meeting or the early morning hour because it would get in the way of their jobs and other responsibilities, but my parents didn't care. They were anxious to see these wrongs made right and they wanted the bully gang's behavior stopped.

Chapter 57

To Walk or Fight

By the time I got home from school I was nervous and uncomfortable thinking about tomorrow's meeting. It was going to be a face off between my team, which included Megan, me, our parents and the Miltons' lawyer, against Devlin, Kevin, Jenni, Deidre, Debbie and all of their parents, as well as Jeffrey's dad. Yes, the principal felt that Jeffrey's involvement in all of this made it impossible to leave his parents out of the meeting, but my mom told me that Jeffrey's mom wouldn't be coming.

I thought it would do me good to stop thinking about the meeting (my mom always says worrying doesn't help anything), so I called Charlie.

"Hey, can you come out?" I asked.

"Glove?"

"Yes, of course."

* * *

"Stephen, did I hear right?" Charlie said, tossing the ball.

"Not unless you heard left." I laughed.

"I get it, that's not funny."

"Okay, probably not," I said, but I kept laughing anyway.

Charlie waited until I stopped before speaking.

"So are you really meeting with the whole bully gang?" he asked.

"Yep, all of them." I tried to make it sound like it was no big deal.

"You really know how to make life hard on yourself don't you."

"I had to do it."

"Why? You've been doing so well tucking tail and running."

"Yeah, I'm tired of running."

"Well if you had listened to me years ago you would have just clobbered them upside their heads and they would have left you alone then."

"Diplomacy."

"Yeah, that's what people say who have never been bullied."

"That's probably true but it's still the right thing to do."

"Maybe."

"No maybe. Would you rather fight someone and risk getting punched in the nose or shake hands and walk away?" I asked.

"When you give me these hypothetical questions why do you always use the nose? You know the thought of getting hit in the nose freaks me out."

"That's why I do it, worst case scenario."

"Okay, so the nose or shake hands?"

"Yes."

"Did he pick his nose first?"

"What?"

"Did he pick his nose, because if he picked his nose then I am not shaking his hand."

"He didn't pick his nose," I said, rolling my eyes.

"Okay, if I put my hand out he's not going to just pull his away is he?"

"No, why would he do that?"

"Because he's a jerk and that's probably why I wanted to fight him to begin with."

"You're not actually fighting anyone."

"Then why are you asking me these stupid questions?"

"Oh my gosh!" I said, circling my finger at the side of my head. "Nuts!"

"No thanks, I don't like nuts. Nuts and vegetables I can live without."

"No, *you're* nuts, but that reminds me of something I've been meaning to ask you. I saw you and Peggy Sloan talking at lunch the other day. What's up with that? I thought you said it was over?"

"I thought I would give her a second chance."

"Really, and how did it go?"

"It went much better."

"It did?"

"Yeah, it did."

"What was with the sunglasses?"

"I put them on so I can talk to her."

"What?" I couldn't even imagine what he meant.

"The glasses are dark enough that I can't see the food stuck in her teeth," Charlie explained. He stood up taller when he said this, like he was proud of himself.

"So, you're going to date her wearing sunglasses every time she eats?"

"That's my thinking."

"What happens if she wants to come over to your house for dinner?"

"What?"

"You're going to wear sunglasses at your mom's dinner table?"

"I never thought of that."

"Don't you think you should?"

"I'm in trouble," Charlie said. Then, in a panicked voice, "I gotta go."

"Where are you going?"

"I have to break up with Peggy," Charlie said as he ran into his house.

Chapter 58

A Stranger Calls

When I went back inside I heard the phone ring. My dad took the call, and as I watched the expressions change on his face, I could only wonder who was on the other end. He didn't say much, but he listened and said "yes", "no" and "I understand" a lot. The last thing he said before he hung up was, "Sure, we'll see you in a few minutes."

I looked at my dad and raised my eyebrows, meaning it like "Who was that?", but he looked a little uneasy and didn't say anything to me. Still, I wasn't surprised when I heard someone knocking on the door a few minutes later and I went to answer it. Now I was surprised. Mr. Talin was standing there. I don't think he's any older than my dad, but right then he looked like he could be ten years older. His hair was short and mostly grey and when he looked up to greet me, his face looked tired and sad.

"Hi, Stephen," he said.

"Mr. Talin," I said with surprise.

"Your dad said it was alright if I stopped by."

"Sure, come in. I'll get him."

"That's okay, I'm actually here to see you. Your dad and I talked about it when I called."

"Oh ... um, okay, but why me?" I felt the sudden need to be anywhere else but standing there.

"Can we sit?" Mr. Talin asked.

"Sure." I led him inside.

When you come in through the front door of my house you're right in the middle of our living room, so we didn't have far to go to find a seat. The room is painted yellow, which makes it look really bright and comfortable, and my mom keeps potpourri on a table so it smells really good. There is a small couch as soon as you walk in, with its back facing the entrance, and a larger matching one against the wall, facing the TV and windows that look out on our side yard. There are a lot of family photos on top of the TV cabinet and Mr. Talin glanced at them as he sat down on the edge of the small couch. I sat facing him, on the big couch, as he started to talk.

"I want to talk to you about Jeffrey," Mr. Talin said.

"Mr. Talin, I am so sorry. I liked Jeffrey, he made me laugh," I blurted out. I really had no idea what to say.

"I am very glad to hear that, though it's going to make it harder for me to say some of the things I need to say."

"What things?"

"Do you know that Jeffrey was trying to get you suspended from school?"

"I know now, but I didn't know before he died."

"Have you been receiving things in the mail?"

"Yes."

"Did you know that Jeffrey was involved with that too?"

"I actually only found out about that a little before he died."

Mr. Talin nodded. "I'm sorry, Stephen. I don't know what was going on in his head. He was always such a good kid."

"I think he just wanted to fit in. Isn't that really all any of us wants, just to fit in? I know that's what I want, so I can understand what he was thinking."

"But he went about it the wrong way and I guess that's why I came here tonight. I want to try to help make it right. Will you let me do that?" Mr. Talin's voice sounded almost pleading.

"I'm not sure I understand," I said.

"My wife and I were horrified when we discovered what Jeffrey had been doing with those kids. No one should have to endure that kind of treatment, and I want to help you put a stop to it. I don't have any reason to attend this parent meeting tomorrow, at least not on behalf of Jeffrey. There is nothing I can say that will defend his behavior and I wouldn't even try to defend it if he were alive. But I do want to be there for you, I want you to know that. I would be grateful if you'd let me help you, but I want your permission. If you tell me to get lost right now I will understand and there will be no hard feelings."

"How can you help me?"

"You let me worry about that. I just wanted to make sure that, knowing what you know about Jeffrey, you're okay with me being there for you tomorrow."

"Sure, I can use all the help I can get."

"Well, I appreciate you letting me, it might help me sleep better." Mr. Talin stood up to leave.

"Thank you," I said.

"No, thank you."

Chapter 59

Jeffrey Speaks

Mr. Heftler entered the conference room shutting the door behind him. This room has a much different feel to it than his office. There are no photos or knickknacks around the room to give it character. It's just a big white room with a very long table in the center surrounded by lots of metal and hard plastic chairs. There are a few windows on one wall but the blinds are shut so we can't see out. I'm not sure but I think you'd look out at the playground if they were open.

Me and my parents were the first to arrive and I don't mind saying that I was getting a little nervous. Facing the bully gang and their parents all together in one room was starting to seem like a bad idea and it wasn't until Jeffrey's dad got here that I began to relax a little.

Mr. Heftler told my parents he expects the meeting to be a short one, but he promised them that the message will be powerful. I don't know what he has in mind but I hope it works. Mr. Heftler looked around the room to get a quick head count and then tried to get people's attention.

"Excuse me everyone, are we all situated?" Not really waiting for an answer, he continued, "Great, so let's get started. I want to tell you all that I truly appreciate you coming in this morning to support your kids. What I'm hoping is that everyone will listen to what is discussed today with an open mind. I don't know if all of you are acquainted with Mr. Talin, but this is Jeffrey's father. Mr. Talin came to me with information about what has been taking place between your children and Stephen Miller. After hearing Mr. Talin out, I knew the information he had brought me is vital to getting this situation straightened out and he has agreed to share with all of you today what he has already shared with me. So for now I am going to turn the floor over to Mr. Talin."

"Thanks, Principal Heftler." Mr. Talin looked around the table at everyone before continuing. "I don't know if you can imagine what it's like to loose a child, but if you can, then you'll know how painful it is for me to speak in front of you today. My wife and I have had our eyes opened, we have had to reexamine everything we thought was true about our son Jeffrey in order to try to understand what happened to him. In doing this we found pain we didn't know existed, both in him and in us. We found truths that we could only hope were lies, only to find our hopes shattered.

A few years ago Jeffrey decided it would be fun to keep a journal. I would like to read to you some of his private entries from that journal, but before I do, I just want to say one thing: Parents, the first thing your kids are going to do is either try to spin this problem in their best interests or deny it. My suggestion for all of you is to believe nothing they tell you and just look for the truth."

Mr. Talin picked up what must have been Jeffrey's journal from the table.

"Please keep in mind that these are Jeffrey's words. In an entry from May, *Jenni gave me a list of CDs to send to Stephen.*"

When Jenni heard her name she jumped up from her chair like she got stung in the butt by a bee.

"That is a lie!" Jenni screamed. "A total lie!"

"Jenni, enough," her dad said, trying to get her to sit back down. "Calm down, it's just about a list of CDs."

"It's just not true!" Jenni insisted.

"Jenni, please stop," said Mr. Heftler. "And Parents, please try to keep your children from acting out like this. This is important! I have read Jeffrey's journal and, after reading it, I thought it was important to share with you. As for you students, there are going to be things said here that you are not going to like, but if anyone of you calls out again, I will remove you from this room and just let your parents listen. Is that clear?" Mr. Heftler looked around the room. No one responded. "I'm sorry, Mr. Talin, continue."

"In another May entry, *Deidre thought the Liberace CD was the best choice and Kevin agreed so we sent Liberace. I thought it was the funniest too, ha,ha,ha!*"

Mr. Talin stopped reading. Deidre and Kevin were both mumbling "lie" loud enough for everyone to hear. Mr. Heftler turned in their direction but their parents told them to stop. When it seemed that things were under control again, Mr. Talin continued.

"Still in May, Jeffrey wrote, *Debbie and Kevin dropped off the*

Virginia Seeds catalog. Then, in an entry from June, *Sent the pansies and pussy willow seeds to Stephen. I guess those were the right ones since they were the only ones they checked off.* Actually, the rest of these that I'll be reading are all from June entries. One says, *Devlin and Kevin were giving me a hard time today because they didn't think the seeds were sent, but I checked and they were.* Another, a few days later says, *Today Kevin suggested that I come up with better ideas and said what we were doing isn't working. He said he would love to see Stephen kicked off the baseball team. Got an idea when Kevin said that only serious cheating, like copying a term paper, could get him kicked off. Didn't tell Kevin my idea. I want to surprise Devlin.*"

"That's crap!" said Kevin. "It's just crap."

Kevin's father's face turned beet red from embarrassment. He turned to Kevin and, sounding angry said, "What did you say?"

"I said it was crap, it's all lies," Kevin answered.

"Mr. Longley, I think your son should leave the room," said Mr. Heftler.

"Jim, I think he should stay. I don't want him to be able to walk away from this. Please side with me here," said Mr. Longley, pleading.

"Okay, I understand your position," said Mr. Heftler. Then, shaking his head, he said, "I'm sorry for the interruption, Mr. Talin."

Mr. Talin continued, "As I said, the remainder of the entries are all from June. One says, *The Lewis and Clark essay is done and copied. Bought binders in every color for Stephen's new essay.*

And another, *I switched essays on Stephen. It wasn't as hard as I thought. Devlin and Kevin were watching and are excited. They said I did good and even invited me to play basketball with them.*"

Every time Mr. Talin read Kevin's name Kevin moaned and rolled his eyes, but he didn't have another outburst. That's probably because his dad had his hand on Kevin's shoulder to remind him he was there. When Kevin spoke out the first time and Mr. Heftler said he could stay, Mr. Longley leaned over and whispered something to Kevin. I don't know what he said, but Kevin turned pale. I guess that's what's keeping him quiet now.

Mr. Talin was still reading, "*Mom and Dad got a call from Miss Stanton who wants to talk to them about my essay. Meeting tomorrow morning.* Then, the rest of these entries are all from the same day. First, *Plagiarism! I have been suspended for plagiarism? It can't be true. Please! Oh no, it can't be. I don't know what happened and I can't tell the truth. I don't know what to do.* Then, *Devlin and Kevin threatened me, said if I say anything my life won't be worth living. Devlin slammed me into a locker before I left school and said get used to it. NOOOOO! This can't be happening.* The next one says, *My mom and dad are screaming and they think I plagiarized the essay, but I didn't. I told them I didn't do it, but I can't tell them the truth. I want to just tell them, but how can I? The truth is worse than the lie.* And then, the last two: *Mom and Dad, I love you. I am sorry.* and *Stephen, I am so, so sorry!*"

Mr. Talin read the last line looking right at me.

"That's it," said Mr. Talin. He put the journal down. Then he looked at me again and said, "Stephen, I just want to tell you that my wife and I are deeply sorry as well."

"Thank you," I said.

The room was quiet after that and most everyone looked like they had just been swatted in the face with a tennis racket. No one seemed to know what to say, or even wanted to speak for that matter. I had to admit my heart jumped when I heard my name mentioned in Jeffrey's journal. He said he was sorry and I just wanted to tell him, "It's okay, I understand." A minute later the silence in the room was replaced with the sound of Mr. Heftler's voice.

"I know what Mr. Talin read to you was hard to hear, and I don't want to rub salt in the wound, but this was only a small fraction of what Jeffrey recorded in his journal over the last year," said Mr. Heftler.

"There's more?" asked Mr. Longley. "How much more?"

"About eight months worth," Mr. Heftler replied.

"We were told you had some kind of evidence," said Deidre's mom. "Is this journal it?"

"We also have tangible evidence of bullying that Mr. Miller has provided us in the manner of inappropriate notes and letters, among other things," Mr. Heftler responded.

"When can we see that?" Deidre's mom asked.

"All of that information will be provided, but not during this meeting," said Mr. Heftler.

"When?" asked Mr. Longley.

"Parents, my suggestion at this point, to avoid any further emotional outbursts, is to take your children home and look over

the materials in the folders that I have given each family. These folders contain all the information you're asking for."

"Do we need a lawyer?" asked Mr. Longley.

"That is up to you," said Mr. Heftler.

"I don't have the money for an attorney," said Debbie's mom.

"Parents, please, go home. Review the packets and then call the office in the morning to set up an appointment to meet privately. I will need speak with each family separately anyway, and at that time we can go over any questions you might have. If you feel you want to get your attorney involved, that is fine, you can bring them along to your meeting. It is my hope that we can clear this situation up as quickly as possible," Mr. Heftler said.

I don't know if you noticed this or not, but Devlin and his parents sat quietly in the back row and didn't say a word during this whole meeting. They didn't object or question anything, and Devlin didn't groan or make any comments. They just listened. I don't know that this means anything, but I thought it was interesting how Devlin's troops went up in a blaze while he sat silently in the shadows. I have seen plenty of Mafia movies and I think that is exactly what the big bad Mafioso boss would have done too.

I looked at Megan from time to time during the meeting and she looked preoccupied, but it wasn't until it was over that I realized why. For Megan, Jeffrey's death was on her and the only way to get it off was to face it head on. So when the meeting was done Megan did what she came here to do: apologize.

I don't think Mr. Talin was prepared for Megan's apology because he looked surprised when she first approached him. But he listened without comment while she talked, and then he said some things to her, and then leaned over and gave her a hug. Anyone watching her right then could see how relieved she was, and Megan walked away able to leave her guilt behind.

Chapter 60

Consequences

When the meeting was over Megan and I both went to our classes. We had missed a couple by now, but there wasn't a lot going on with it being the last day of school anyway. Kids were talking and signing yearbooks and comparing plans for summer vacations. All in all it was a peaceful end to what had been a pretty rough year.

None of the bully gang stuck around after the meeting. Their parents whisked them right out the front doors and away they went. I couldn't help wondering which ones were going to be in trouble and which ones not so much. If I had been one of the bullies, my parents would have killed me, but not all parents are the same.

I didn't see Megan the rest of the day because we didn't have our last two classes on half days. I wondered if she'd be in any of my classes next year. You never know from year to year who'll end up in class with you, but I hoped we'd be together.

When the last bell rang I waited outside for Megan. I saw Jack waving at me from inside the bus with Charlie sitting right next to him. Charlie and I usually rode home together but since I started walking with Megan he was having fun tormenting Jack.

As I watched the last bus pull away I looked around. I was the only one left out front. I was about to go in and look for Megan when she came out of the school.

"What took you so long?" I asked. "I was starting to think you weren't coming."

"Sorry, I had to meet with Mr. Heftler and then run back to my locker," Megan said.

"Why did you have to meet with Mr. Heftler?"

"He had to give me this," Megan said, holding up a large manila envelope.

"What is it?"

"It's part of my punishment."

"Punishment for what!" I said, sounding surprised.

"For going in Jeffrey's locker."

"You're kidding me, right?"

"Not kidding."

I couldn't believe it.

"The bully gang gets to go home and flip through their folders and you get punished *today*. It doesn't seem right," I said.

"It's okay, what I did was wrong. I can live with the consequences."

"What are the consequences?"

"I have to help at the school this summer."

"Doing what?"

"Helping the teachers with the kids."

"Helping them do what?"

"I'll be tutoring some of the kids who need extra help. Who knows, it might actually be fun," Megan said.

"Who are you going to be tutoring?"

"They gave me a choice. I can work with Mrs. Fleck, who has the second and third graders, or with Mrs. Balkco's kids. The other choice is to work one-on-one with the same student each day for two hours."

"Did they tell you what student?"

"They did."

"Who?"

"I had a choice between Shane and Dwayne Sullivan."

"No way! I hope you took the kids in Mrs. Fleck's class."

"I did, actually, but Mr. Heftler decided that he would rather me work one-on-one."

"So you had to choose between Shane or Dwayne?"

"I told Mr. Heftler I couldn't choose."

"So what did he say?"

"He said if I couldn't pick then he would have to choose for me."

"And who did he choose?"

"I don't know, he handed me this envelope and said to look it over when I got home."

"Do you know what's in it?"

"I guess it's the name of the student and a list of all the work he needs help with," Megan said.

"So open it and see which one you got. I hope it's not Shane."

I leaned closer to Megan so I could see better when she opened the envelope, but she handed it to me instead.

"You open it and tell me which one it is," Megan said.

"You sure?"

"Yes, open it."

I opened the clasp on the back of the envelope and took out the papers from inside. I read the name of the student Megan would be tutoring this summer and tried not to laugh.

"Out of all the people in the school, why would Mr. Heftler give you him?" I asked.

"Who is it?" Megan tried to look at the papers I was holding.

"Stephen Miller."

"What?" Megan said, looking confused.

"He has assigned you me," I said, smiling.

"No way!"

"Yes way."

"That's worse than the Sullivan brothers," said Megan. Now she was smiling too.

"Hey, that's not nice."

"I'm kidding!"

"What kind of punishment is that anyway?" I said.

"Mr. Heftler just said that instead of someone else doing it, I will be spending two hours each day helping you get caught up."

"So you knew?"

"Of course I did. Do you really think he would give me the Sullivan brothers to tutor?"

"It did sound a little strange," I admitted.

"Just a little?"

"Well, it *was* supposed to be a punishment. That definitely would have qualified. But you're going to help me, huh?"

"Yep. It's you and me, so you better buckle down and do your work."

"Does Mr. Heftler know that you broke into my locker too?"

"I don't think so, why?"

"Maybe I should tell him."

"Why would you do that?"

"Well, if I get you for two hours for one locker, maybe he'll up it to four for the second B and E."

"B and E?"

"Breaking in and entering."

"How about we just do two hours at the school and then go to my house and swim?" Megan suggested.

"That works too," I agreed.

"So it'll be two hours of hard labor a day," said Megan smiling.

"Yeah, I think that's only fair considering your recent crime wave."

"Really, you consider that a crime wave?"

"In Lamington, it's a crime wave."

Chapter 61

Hard Labor

One thing you learn if you watch enough crime shows on TV is that the bad guy sometimes goes free. So after the bully gang's attorneys all went home and the smoke cleared, not everyone's punishment fit their crime.

Devlin, as it turned out, had kept enough distance between himself and the others that there was no real proof that he participated in any way. Jeffrey's diaries were considered hearsay (which I've learned means information that comes from a source that can't be "verified" -- which I learned means confirmed), so without one of the bully gang coming forward and speaking out against him there wasn't any real evidence against Devlin. He was a free man.

The rest of the bully gang wasn't so lucky though. They all were caught red-handed with their hands in the cookie jar and it got slammed shut. For their part in the bullying, Kevin, Deidre and the others were all sentenced to hard time at summer school with Mr. Flemming. Mr. Flemming is a tough old guy with a crabby attitude and a three-day shadow that makes him look mad all the time. He's the head of Lamington Public School's custodial staff and he put

the gang immediately to work, laying down mulch around the new playground equipment and mopping and scrubbing the hallways and lockers. Charlie said he saw them just yesterday cleaning and painting the school bathrooms.

As you all know, Megan is doing hard time at the school with me. I got a C on my Lewis and Clark essay but it didn't bring my grade up much. Even if it had I wasn't getting out of summer school. But this year it's not so bad. Between Mrs. Balkco and Megan I'm catching up, and actually having some fun doing it too. If you believe the rumors, I will be moving up to eighth grade next year after all.

Speaking of rumors, do you remember the one about Linda Mohoney doing community service hours at the school? Well, turns out it's true. For the first time in recent history my mom got something right. Linda Mohoney is working in the school office a few hours a week to get her hours. Charlie was so excited when he heard the news that he signed up as an office volunteer himself. Mrs. Calvin, the office secretary, was so happy to have two people helping out this year. To make sure there's enough work for both of them, though, she scheduled them to work in alternate shifts. So Linda shows up at 8:30 each morning to work her two hours and then Charlie comes in after lunch. With only two days left of summer school, Charlie has not seen Linda even once. I have to admit I thought it sounded like a good plan when Charlie volunteered, but just like in baseball, sometimes you swing and miss.

Jack is finishing out the baseball season with a record number of swings and misses too. If he goes zero for whatever tonight against the Cardinals he will have struck out every single at bat this season. Guinness Book has been put on notice.

In spite of a rough game or two, my baseball season has been more hits than misses and the Giants finished the regular season with a record of 13 wins and 3 losses. The only team we really had to worry about all season was Devlin's Cardinals, who tied us for the best record. Because of the tie though we now have to play them in a divisional playoff game, with the winner moving on to the next level, and one step closer to the Little League World Series.

Chapter 62

Win or Go Home

Cardinals vs. Giants

The only thing that brings more people to the ball field than opening day is a good playoff game. The lights are on, the players are all introduced as they run onto the field and the whole thing feels like you're in a movie. It's really cool to be one of those players under the lights, with the excitement of the crowd surrounding you and the dirt under your feet. You can smell the fresh cut grass in the night air and the burgers frying at the snack shack. You look into the bleachers and see your family and friends and you feel this nervous energy flow through your body. You take that energy and hold onto it because it gives you the edge and helps keep you sharp.

For me that energy is never stronger than when I am on deck in the hitting circle. I know my time at bat is coming and I'm anticipating it, rooting for the player at bat to get on already so I can have my turn. It's even worse when the bases are loaded and there's only one out because mathematically I know I should get up, but that's only going to happen if the person at the plate doesn't hit into a double play.

And that is where we are now right now. The bases are loaded with one out and we're down by two runs with a new batter at the plate. The whole season comes down to right here and now, and from the on deck circle all I can do is take a deep breath and keep my fingers crossed.

* * *

"Who's up?" says Megan as she sits down next to Charlie in the stands.

"Why are you back so soon? I told you this is the best time to go," says Charlie.

"I forgot my purse, it's fine. Who's up?"

"Jack."

"Oh, good. I told you I want to see him bat."

"Why, you like strikeouts?"

"Stop, he could get a hit."

"Right, that's going to happen," Charlie says sarcastically. "If he strikes out here this will be his 48th strikeout of the season."

"Stephen's been working with him."

"Tell him not to give up his day job."

"You're terrible."

* * *

I have been practicing with Jack but his love for that high fastball is hard to break. "Come on Jack, let's get a hit," I yell for encouragement. Jack has been hitless all season and will set a league record for strikeouts if he goes down swinging again. Jack called Guinness weeks ago but they never got back to him. He was disappointed. He really was looking forward to having his name in the record books with Reggie Jackson.

* * *

"Come on Jack, get a hit!" yells Charlie.

"I thought you didn't root?" asks Megan.

"Devlin's pitching, I root against him every game," Charlie explains. "Come on, Jack!" he screams even louder.

* * *

Devlin is a tough pitcher to hit and tonight he has been dead-on accurate all game long. I led off the first inning with a single and then stole second but was stuck there twiddling my thumbs for the rest of the inning. Our only run came in the fourth when I sent Devlin's fastball over the left field fence, taking out someone's front windshield in the parking lot (you would think people would learn not to park there). Our pitcher, Dell, gave up three runs in the first but has been solid since. So here we are, bottom of the seventh, and we finally have a little life back in us, a little hope. That nervous energy is overflowing in all of us. If Jack just stays away from the high fast..."

"Oh Jaaaack, don't swing at those! Come on, don't help him,"

I say, hopefully loud enough for him to hear.

Jack steps out of the box and calls for time out. He is messing with his gloves again. This is his new ritual and he is sticking to it. He says if it works for Jeter then maybe it will work for him. Baseball players are a superstitious bunch, but you can't really argue with his logic. Jack takes a couple swings and then steps back into the box.

"Play ball," the umpire yells.

Jack looks at Devlin and watches his head shake yes, and just as it looks like he might move Jack calls for another time out and steps out of the box.

"Time," yells the umpire.

Jack peels the straps back on his batting gloves again, then tightens them to his wrists. He takes another two swings and moves back into the batter's box. He watches Devlin shake off a couple of signs, then Devlin goes into his wind up and delivers another high fastball.

*   *   *

"Nooooo, Jack, stop swinging at those!" Charlie yells.

"Why does he swing at those?" Megan asks.

"I have no idea," Charlie says, baffled. "He's been doing it as long as I can remember."

"Come on Jack, you can do it!" Megan yells.

*   *   *

Devlin is on the mound kicking at the dirt in front of the rubber as Jack steps back into the batter's box for what seems like the hundredth time. I know Jack keeps calling time to try to prepare himself mentally for Devlin's pitches. He's been trying to watch for the ball coming out of the pitcher's hand like I told him to do. I give him credit for trying.

When Devlin goes into his windup, Jack is dug in and ready. With the count 0 and 2, Devlin comes at Jack with everything he's got, but this time it's not Jack's favorite pitch buzzing toward him at rapid speed. This fastball is the knockout punch, destined to cross the plate in the middle of the strike zone; the perfect pitch. As the ball speeds toward the plate, Jack's eyes grow wide and he lets the bat loose on the ball.

The crack of the bat brings everyone to their feet and we watch the ball fly off the bat. The screaming and cheering explodes from the crowd as we continue to watch. Jack just stands at home plate, watching in disbelief like the rest of us.

From the moment Jack hits the ball we're all holding our breath. We watch in amazement as it soars across the sky like a shooting star. It's not a give-me shot, so we don't dare celebrate too early, but when the ball clears the center field fence, our team rushes out of the dugout and onto the infield.

Jack doesn't need a kick-start to get moving this time. He is so excited to see the ball go over the fence that he is jumping in the air and running at the same time. As I watch him bounce around the bases, I'm cheering for him as loud as I can. I look in the stands and I see Megan and Charlie yelling and whistling with their arms in the air. I spot my mom, who looks like she's crying, and my dad is clapping and shouting with everyone else. You can actually feel the excitement, and it's amazing!

I'm still cheering, but as I'm watching Jack run, I can't help but laugh. With all his bouncing, Jack is doing a pretty good imitation of Tigger and looks a lot like a pogo stick with a hat. I wait proudly at home plate with my arms stretched open and Jack leaps in the air for me to catch. The whole team tackles us into the dirt and it feels good. Maybe not as good as if I had hit the grand slam myself, but pretty darn good.

On the other side of the field I see the Cardinals and their fans. You can tell by the expressions on their faces that they're all devastated, and some of them aren't afraid to show it. You can hear a few swear words and players crying. I even watch one kid throw his glove in the dirt. But then I see Devlin and he isn't doing any of those things. With my team celebrating at home plate, Delvin is still standing on the mound in shock. I know that in Devlin's mind Jack is a joke. He has been considered the easiest out in baseball for years, so I think it's safe to say that Devlin's worst case scenario for how this game -- heck, this season! -- could end just smacked him in the face and said *GOTCHA! Good guys win!*

The one thing I know about sports is nothing is certain. You can lay out every scenario you can think of and the one that never crossed your mind slips under the door. Jack finished the season with 47 strikeouts and 1 hit, and who knows what will happen during the rest of the playoffs, but at the end of it all, I think my coach just summed it up best when he said it doesn't always take a lot to leave a big impression.

Chapter 63

The Silver Lining

Did I ever tell you that having my best friend right across the street is the greatest thing ever? Well, it is.

* * *

I pick up the phone and dial. I don't even think of the numbers because my fingers know them by heart.

"Can you come out?" I say.

"Be right there. Glove?"

"Absolutely."

* * *

"What took you so long?" I ask when Charlie finally comes out of the house. "I've been standing here forever."

"Peggy called as I was leaving."

"Peggy Sloan?"

"Yeah."

"I thought you broke it off with her?"

"I was going to."

"So why didn't you?"

"You know that show 'America's Next Supermodel'?"

"Yes," I say. I have no idea where this is going.

"My mom loves that show."

"What does this have to do with Peggy?"

"When I ran in the house the other day my mom was watching it."

"Again, soooo?"

"Well, they showed a picture of one the contestants when she was in school."

"Yeah?"

"In her school photo she looked just like Peggy."

"Really?"

"They could be twins."

"So you're thinking Peggy will eventually look like this supermodel on TV?"

"Exactly! How can I break up with a supermodel, people will laugh at me." Charlie says this completely seriously.

"I'm laughing at you now!" I say.

"Stephen, look at me. I look like an albino with light orange hair. This could be my only chance to ever date a supermodel."

"You do realize that Peggy turning into a supermodel is crazy and very unlikely?"

"I thought your brother just getting a hit was unlikely and look what happened there."

"That is true," I admit.

"I talked to your brother yesterday, you know."

"Good for you."

"He said that you're jealous."

"He didn't say that."

"He did," Charlie insists.

"I know he didn't."

"How do you know?"

"Because it's coming from your lips, that's why."

"Are you insinuating that I'm lying?"

"No, I am *saying* that you're lying."

"Well, as long as you're not insinuating it."

I stop throwing the ball and look at Charlie. "Megan's right, there is something very wrong with you."

"Stephen, let's be serious, you're not at least a little jealous?"

"I'm not."

"Stop, you are too."

"I'm not," I say.

"Come on, even I'm jealous."

"Well *you* should be."

"Why should I be jealous?"

"You've never hit a home run, let alone a walk-off to win a playoff game."

"That's true. Now I'm really jealous."

"You should be happy for him," I say.

"Why is that?"

"Because I am." And I really am.

"I don't care if you're happy, you're always happy."

"That's not true and you know it."

"Stephen, you got the girl, you win the games and you took down the bully gang. One day you'll be playing for the Yankees while I'm watching you on TV. You'll be in your mansion playing Xbox with some supermodel girlfriend while I am sitting at home with Peggy Sloan. Tell me you don't see the silver lining ending to your story?"

"Charlie, what I see is that things don't always turn out according to plan. Now stop thinking so much and play ball." Then I threw the ball back to Charlie with a little extra zip on it.

Wzzzzzzzzzzzzzzzzzzzzzzzz, POP!

"Owwwwwwwwwwww! Stephen!"

"You see, Charlie? You didn't plan on *that* did you?" And I bust out laughing.

About the author:

Daryl Cobb lives in New Jersey with his family, not far from his childhood hometown. Daryl's writing began in college as a Theatre Arts major at Virginia Commonwealth University. He found a freshman writing class inspiring and, combined with his love for music and the guitar, he discovered a passion for songwriting. This talent would motivate him for years to come and the rhythm he created with his music also found its way into the bedtime stories he later created for his children. Through the years his son and daughter have inspired much of his work, including "Boy on the Hill", "Daniel Dinosaur" and "Daddy Did I Ever Say? I Love You, Love You, Every Day".

When Daryl isn't writing or plucking on his guitar he is visiting schools promoting literacy with his interactive educational assemblies. Daryl is one of New Jersey's premier educational performers whose use of performance arts to teach and entertain has educators and assembly coordinators everywhere consistently calling his school programs "the best of the best." These performance programs teach children about the writing and creative processes and allow Daryl to do what he feels is most important -- inspire children to read and write.

Made in the USA
Middletown, DE
10 April 2019